Hot Tub of Death

(A Sunshine Valley Mystery)

by

Rita Strombeck

Copyright 2014 by Rita Strombeck

For information, email **Cozy Cat Press**, cozycatpress@aol.com or visit our website at: www.cozycatpress.com

COZY CAT
PRESS

ISBN: 978-1-939816-39-9

Printed in the United States of America

Cover design by Karri Klawiter
http://artbykarri.com/cover-art/e-book-print-cover-art-design/

1 2 3 4 5 6 7 8 9 10

For my parents, Elof and Karin, who introduced
me to Arizona and always supported my
writing

Chapter 1

Most evenings, the setting of the sun on the Sonoran desert is followed by hours of quiet solitude, but this was not going to be one of those evenings. From the moment she settled into bed, Eve Iverson was distracted from *German For Travelers* by the sound of a neighbor, one Olive Howell to be exact, who was screaming at her husband Frank. This was not an unusual event. However, this time, the shouting was louder and lasted longer.

"I can't believe that woman. She's nuts. I think we should call the police," Eve pleaded to her husband Adam.

"Somebody probably already has," he mumbled.

"I hope you're right." But, Eve was doubtful that anyone would bother, or even dare, to report the disturbance. *No one had done so in the past and it was unlikely the situation would be any different tonight,* she thought.

After another fifteen minutes of being subjected to the neighbor's rampage, Eve lost all remaining patience and slammed her book shut. Hostility was not a feeling she experienced very often, but, periodically, it would surface, especially if the focus of her anger was someone who was abusing or taking advantage of others. Such was the case this evening.

"I can't take any more of this. It's almost ten o'clock. Call the police," Eve commanded to the head bobbing up and down at the foot of the bed.

"In a minute. Sixty-two ...Sixty-three ... Sixty-four... Sixty-five... Sixty-six." Adam jumped up, exhaled, and puffed out his chest. "There," he proudly exclaimed, "I'm finished."

"Good," replied Eve. "That's one for each year. *Now*, will you call the police? Or, if you're not going to do it, I will." Her tone left no room for refusal.

"Why?" Adam asked, as he began flinging his arms back and forth across his chest. Few things in life bothered him, and a noisy neighbor was not one of them.

"What do you mean *why*? Are you deaf? Haven't you heard what's been going on for the past few hours?" Eve was losing what little patience she still maintained.

Adam ignored his wife's exasperation and calmly replied, "She's stopped."

And so she had. As suddenly as it had begun, the neighbor's tirade had come to an abrupt end.

"I don't believe it. Now that she's managed to disturb the entire neighborhood with her ranting and raving, she's probably exhausted and ready for a good night's sleep. Or, even better, maybe Frank finally put her out of her misery."

Eve rolled out from underneath the warm down cover, put on her slippers and blue wool robe and walked over to the door that opened onto the patio. She slid back the heavy glass pane and shuddered as the chilly March air rushed in. All around, there was nothing but darkness and total silence. Far off in the distance, a tiny light blinked on and off, slowly making its way across the black sky, as silent as the night itself. The smell of mesquite burning in neighboring fireplaces filled the air. Wagging its tail, the couple's French poodle followed Eve and lifted its head, eagerly awaiting instructions. "Stay inside, Coco. It's too cold out there," she said as she bent down and patted the dog's curly black head.

As she pulled the door shut, Eve continued looking out at the silent sky for a few minutes, then turned towards Adam, almost embarrassed by her impatience, now that the familiar desert silence had returned. "It's really amazing how clearly we could hear her, even with the door closed," Eve said apologetically. "It must be the wind. It's very strong tonight and probably carried her voice this way."

Adam nodded in agreement, but said nothing. Noticing the look of distress on his face, Eve felt a sudden desire to comfort her husband. *How considerate he could be at times,* she thought, *and yet, so impetuous on other occasions.* Even though it wasn't her idea initially, in the end, she supported Adam's desire to leave California when they retired and make the move to Arizona. He had worked as a hospital administrator in San Diego most of his adult life and, one year, was asked to attend a professional meeting in Tucson. To his great surprise, he immediately fell in love with the desert and knew that was where he was going to live some day.

Despite the fact that the couple had owned a home by the ocean and, for many years, enjoyed leisurely walks along the shore, as soon as they officially retired from work, Adam suggested they check out Arizona. Never one to turn her back on the promise of adventure, Eve kept any doubts she might have to herself. At first, they explored several houses around the Tucson area, then, one day, as they drove south towards the border, they discovered Sunshine Valley. Both Adam and Eve agreed, this town was beautiful and really lived up to its name. Surrounded on all sides by majestic mountains, hardly a day passed without full sun and cloudless blue skies.

They wasted no time and immediately began looking at houses that were for sale in the numerous developments that were emerging in the area. Two in particular caught their eye, but they opted for the one in Vista Verde Estates on Camino Avion. The detached, beige, one-story, three bedroom, Spanish-style stucco house boasted an arched entrance way, a dark, richly carved front door, large picture windows that faced the mountains, and a red tile roof. Adam pointed out that, since it faced west, they would be able to relax on the patio in the evenings, enjoy a cocktail, and watch the colorful sunsets.

After making a down payment, they quickly returned to San Diego, emptied the house they had owned for years, put it up for sale, then packed their car with the merest of personal belongings and returned to Sunshine Valley to begin a new, second life. Now, nearly a year later, they were both comfortably and happily settled in their little paradise, as Adam referred to their new home.

"Stop looking at me like that," said Eve self consciously. Despite her chagrin, she was touched by her husband's concern for her feelings. After forty years of marriage, she appreciated the fact that he still worried about her and always did whatever he could to console her if a problem would arise.

"Like what?" Adam asked, feigning a tone of innocence.

"I can't stand it when you think I'm upset. Maybe I should follow Coco's lead. She usually barks when she hears strange noises, but, by now, after several months of listening to Olive scream, she's so used to it, she doesn't even lift her head. Anyway, it's not your fault that we have a lunatic for a neighbor."

"You're right about that, but I am sorry she upsets you so much. I thought our biggest inconvenience would be the hot weather in summer. It never occurred to me that we might have a problem with neighbors. Dave said they were both such nice folks."

"Dave?" asked Eve.

"Dave Wilcox. You remember him...the man who sold us our house."

"Oh," replied Eve, dismissing his comment with a wave, "realtors are all alike. You know you can't believe everything they say. They're usually just anxious to make a sale and will tell you what they think you want to hear."

"Well, anyway, I am sorry," Adam added sincerely. "I know that Olive can be a bit of a nuisance."

"More than a bit. I think she brings out the worst in others...at least that's the effect she seems to have on me. In any case, something needs to be done. I'll try to have a little talk with her tomorrow. She probably doesn't realize how far her voice travels." Eve sat down on the edge of the bed, picked up her German book and flipped through the pages, trying to find where she'd left off.

"What are you going to say to her?" asked Adam, as he pulled on his robe.

"I don't know yet. I'll take care of it. I'll think of something tactful. Don't you worry." Eve assumed her most reassuring tone, but wondered exactly what she would say to the woman. She didn't like the thought of a confrontation, knowing full well how easily neighbors could become enemies in an instant.

"I'm not worried. I've seen you in action many times and I have the utmost confidence in your ability to handle lunatics." A look of relief spread across his face. "You want to bet that you end up loving this place after all?" he added.

"You know," Eve began to explain, "I may not have the same cowboy fantasies that you have, but I don't dislike it here. I think the desert is fabulous and I love our home."

"It's the boots, isn't it?" Adam asked sheepishly.

"And the Stetson, and the..." Rather than finish her thought, she exclaimed, "Oh, never mind," and started to laugh. "I'm sorry. If you want to play Roy Rogers, I'll gladly be your Dale. Actually, I think you look kind of cute in your outfit."

"Well," sighed Adam, "cute wasn't exactly what I had in mind. You know they wear those things here. It's part of adapting to the local customs."

"I know, dear. Now, why don't you mosey into the kitchen and rustle us up a cup of tea? It's kind of chilly in here and I think hot tea is a local custom that would be perfect right now. After all the commotion, I'm not ready to go to sleep yet." Eve hoped her husband would pick up on the change of subject.

"My thoughts exactly." Without hesitating, Adam turned and left the room.

"Wait. I'm coming too." Eve put her book under her arm and started down the hallway. Wagging her curly tail, the couple's poodle followed close behind.

Because they were unable to have children, Adam and Eve decided early in their marriage that they would create a surrogate family composed of rescue dogs. Over the years, their desire led to the adoption of Bernie the Afghan, Lucy the Cocker Spaniel, and PeeWee the Collie. After PeeWee died, they decided to hold off getting another dog until they knew where they were going to live when they retired. Shortly after settling into their house in Sunshine Valley, they felt it was time to fill the void in their hearts and went to a local animal shelter. According to Eve, as soon as she made eye contact with the two-year-old black female poodle, both their tails started wagging. She and Adam didn't have to look any further and immediately brought Coco home with them.

"By the way," said Eve, as she followed Adam, "I have to admit I'm quite impressed with the number of pushups you can still do. You certainly are in good shape."

"Piece o' cake," replied Adam, puffing out his chest. "Especially when you start counting at 50."

"Well, you have to start somewhere," replied Eve.

"You're so right." They both broke into laughter.

Once in the kitchen, Adam put the kettle on the stove. Eve carefully adjusted the flame, then sat down on her side of the table. "I wonder how Frank can stand it. He must be incredibly patient. Does he ever say anything to you? Doesn't he ever complain?"

"About what?"

"About Olive, about how she yells at him so much. It seems to be a daily event."

"I don't see how he can tolerate her screaming at him so much. It's endless. Nobody should be subjected to that kind of abuse."

"I think he's used to it by now. It's become somewhat of a routine," said Adam as he placed two large cups on the table. He didn't particularly want to talk about Frank, but knew that Eve was curious and would have more questions.

"How long have they been married?" she asked.

"About five years, I think. Second marriage for him, third for her, or maybe fourth. I forgot. I just know that she's made the rounds, as they say. Frank is somewhat withdrawn and doesn't say much, but I got the impression that they were both very lonely and he thought he was very lucky to find her, at least in the beginning."

"Well," replied Eve, putting a teaspoon of sweetener in her cup, "I don't think this marriage is destined to last much longer. How anyone can put up with Olive's howling is beyond me. She really lives up to her name too, doesn't she? Olive Howell. Olive Howl...get it?"

Adam wasn't quite certain how to respond to his wife and thought it best to ignore her word play. He quietly removed the kettle from the stove, poured the water into Eve's cup, then handed her a tea bag. "Here you go, my dear, this should do you good."

"Oh, Adam, thank you. This is perfect," she said, inhaling the aroma of orange spice.

"You know, in a strange way, I think Frank likes her," continued Adam, as he seated himself across from Eve.

"Come on. You can't be serious. Am I missing something? What is there to like? Has he told you he likes her?"

"Not in so many words, but I know that one thing he enjoys doing is fooling her. That seems to give him a great deal of pleasure."

"What does that mean...he likes to fool her? What are you talking about?" Eve looked at her husband to see if he was teasing her.

"Well, you know how she prides herself on being on top of everything that goes on around here. . ."

"All too well."

"Well, Frank told me one day that he likes to hide things from her. It's his way of getting even."

"What kind of things?" asked Eve, raising her head.

"Oh, just little things—glasses, a pair of shoes...whatever. It doesn't matter what it is, but it drives her crazy to think she's misplaced something."

"That's terrible," exclaimed Eve. "Even though I can understand that he needs to do something to maintain his sanity, I don't think it's very nice to play such silly games. Wouldn't it be better to just confront her?"

"What's so terrible?" asked Adam, carefully sipping the hot tea. "I think it's kind of funny."

"How do you know this, anyway?"

"Frank told me."

"I thought you said that he never talks about Olive."

"Well, he hardly ever mentions her," countered Adam.

Eve shook her head in disbelief. She thought she understood her husband quite well after all these years, but, once in awhile, such as now, he surprised her. "Tell me the truth, do you really think it's funny?" she persisted.

"It's his way of coping. It's really quite harmless and it doesn't hurt anybody. It helps him keep his sanity." Adam smiled uncertainly at his wife and offered her a biscuit, which she declined.

"I can't believe you, Adam. It's so childish and even a bit sadistic. I just hate that kind of sneaky prank. I can't believe you think it's funny. Would you do that to me? Would you hide my things? Or, should I ask, have you already done that to me?"

"No, dear. I never have and I never would. I don't have to. You misplace enough stuff by yourself, without any help from me."

"Very amusing! And I suppose you don't misplace things?" Eve was more annoyed than angry and in no mood to hear any more about Frank's practical jokes. She opened her German book and began reading. After a few minutes, she looked up at her husband and smiled. "Well, now, isn't this perfect!" she exclaimed.

"What's that?" Adam asked as he took a bite out of his biscuit.

"Frank 'ist unter den pantofeln'," she said slowly in her best accent.

"I beg your pardon...he's what?"

"Under the slipper! That's the German expression for being henpecked. Frank is under the slipper."

"Really...I wonder what the origin of that one is?" But, Adam was less enthusiastic than his wife about her linguistic discovery and continued eating.

Eve had been a teacher of Spanish and French for thirty years and always wanted to learn German as well. When Adam suggested they take a trip to Germany so he could do some research for his book on stamps, she jumped at the opportunity to learn the new language. Eve was passionate about languages, but she also needed to keep busy. The generally accepted concept of retirement had no appeal for her. As she often said, "if you look up the word 'retirement' in the dictionary, you will see that it usually has many negative connotations. Synonyms include words such as departure, recession, disuse, retreat, seclusion, regression, resignation, withdrawal, etcetera, etcetera, etcetera. There is no synonym to indicate anything positive, optimistic or forward thinking." So, not content to "retire," Eve divided her new found time between learning another language and painting, and both activities kept her very busy.

She continued reading and sipping her tea, when, all of a sudden, the doorbell began ringing, Adam and Eve looked at each other, baffled. Coco was just as surprised and started to bark and run in circles. Who can that be? It's after ten," said Eve. "You answer it. Maybe it's the police."

Adam pushed himself up from the table and headed for the living room. After switching on the lights, he walked across the room to open the front door. Standing under the arch was a woman dressed neatly in a blue running suit. For a moment, they both stared at each other in awkward silence. When the woman tried to smile, she appeared anxious rather than happy. "I'm so sorry to bother you at this hour, but...I saw that your kitchen lights were on, so I figured you were both still up. If it's not convenient, I can always come back another time...maybe tomorrow. I really don't mean to disturb you."

Coco jumped and snapped nervously at the woman.

"Stop it, Coco. Quiet." Adam leaned down and patted the dog's head. "No, you're not disturbing us, Maggie. Come on in," he said to the late night visitor, as he took her by the arm and led her into the living room. He could tell that she had something important on her mind.

Just at that moment, Eve entered the living room. "Maggie, are you okay? Is something wrong?" she asked hesitantly.

"I was just telling Adam I saw your lights on..."

Eve couldn't help but notice the tone of distress in the woman's voice. Maggie Walsh, a single woman in her late fifties, lived down the street and was one of the first persons to welcome the Iversons to Sunshine Valley after they moved in. She was always very upbeat and cheerful and this anxiety was not like anything Eve had seen in her before, and she feared something serious must have happened to the woman.

"Come in. Please, sit down. Why don't you join us. We were just having tea. Can I get you like a cup?" Eve offered.

"Oh no...thank you...perhaps I should come back another time." She nervously rubbed her hands together, but, despite her words, made no attempt to leave.

Sensing that Maggie wanted to speak to her privately, Eve turned to Adam and said, "Dear, I think your TV program is about to start." It was their long-standing cue that signaled the need for an immediate exit. Adam looked at his wife and then remembered the private things that women sometimes have to share with each other.

"Oh yes...you're right. I'll leave you two alone, if you don't mind." Adam excused himself and headed for the back of the house. "Come on, Coco. Let's go watch Animal Planet." The poodle jumped up, wagging her tail and barking as she followed Adam into the den.

"Now, Maggie, why don't you sit down. You seem very upset. Try to relax. Make yourself comfortable. Just take your time and tell me what's on your mind," Eve said in her calmest voice.

"Thank you. You're so kind," the woman said self-consciously, as she walked over to an armchair and gently sat down.

"Are you sure I can't get you something?" Eve asked again. "It's awfully chilly tonight."

"No, really. I'm fine...I won't be long. I just need to talk to you about something."

Eve pulled up a chair to get closer to her guest. Maggie tried to remain calm, but her nervous hands revealed her true feelings. "I'm so upset," she said, as she swayed back and forth in her chair. "I would have waited until morning, but I felt I just had to talk to you and I didn't want anyone to see me coming over here."

"You're trembling, Maggie. Now, take it slowly and tell me what's bothering you." Attempting to calm her neighbor, Eve placed a firm hand on each of the woman's arms.

"It's so awful...I hate this. It's something I find hard to say...it's too dreadful." The woman picked nervously at the arm of her chair as she began to speak.

Although Eve was curious to hear what was troubling Maggie, she knew that any urgency she might express would only upset her further. She wondered what terrible thing had brought her neighbor out into the cold night at such a late hour. What was upsetting her so much that she had such difficulty expressing?

"Calm down, Maggie, and start from the beginning," said Eve in her most reassuring tone. "I can't help you unless you tell me exactly what it is that's troubling you."

"Well," began Maggie, "you know I told you I went to visit my daughter in Minneapolis last week."

"Yes, I remember...you told me. Please...continue."

"Just before I left, I asked my neighbor Pearl Thomas to come over and water my plants while I was gone." Suddenly, the words came pouring out of her. "Ordinarily, I wouldn't want to ask anyone for favors. I hate asking for help from others, but Pearl has always been so friendly to me...not like some of the people here...if you know what I mean. She gives me her paper when she's finished reading it and told me any time I go away, she'd be happy to look after my house. So, when I went to see my daughter, I took her up on her offer and asked her if she wouldn't mind watering my plants. I was only gone for a week and she only had to come in twice. That's all. Twice." Maggie was gaining courage and began to speak faster.

"Yes. I understand. Tell me...did something happen while you were gone?" Eve was anxious for the woman to get to the point.

"I was so grateful for Pearl's help. I even bought her a box of candy to show my appreciation. But, today, I cut some flowers from my garden and was going to put them in that green crystal vase I have. You know which one I mean?"

"Yes. That's a lovely vase," Eve responded. "I've admired it many times."

"Well, so has Pearl. She told me if I ever wanted to get rid of it, she would be happy to take it. Only, it seems she couldn't wait. It's been in my family for generations and I've had it for years...it's priceless." Her voice began to crack. "You can't imagine how upsetting all of this is." The woman leaned closer and whispered, "Pearl Thomas stole my vase."

Eve leaned back, barely able to restrain herself from bursting into laughter. Tightening the belt around her robe, she chose her words carefully, "I can't believe what you're telling me. Did you look everywhere? Are you sure you didn't misplace it? Sometimes I forget where I put things...it's so easy to do."

"No, I'm sure. I've spent the whole day looking for that vase. I looked everywhere, drawers, closets, everywhere...up and down. No...it has to be Pearl. I'm quite certain she stole it," replied Maggie, stressing the word 'stole.' "Can you imagine? And I trusted that woman. You'd think you could trust your own neighbors not to steal from you. I'm so upset. It's making me a wreck and I don't know what to do next." The woman was practically choking on every word.

"Did you say anything to Pearl about the vase? I know you probably wouldn't ask her if she stole it, but did you ask her if she happened to see it when she came to your house?" Eve asked calmly.

"Oh, good heavens, no. I couldn't do that...I really couldn't. It's too embarrassing. If it were just an ordinary vase, I would go out and buy another one, but it's an heirloom. I just don't know what to do...that's why I came to you."

"Me? What can I possibly do?" Eve asked startled. Suddenly, she realized the purpose of her neighbor's visit.

Maggie's face looked strained. "You'll help me...I know you will. You're friendly with Pearl. You've been to her house. She likes you."

"Yes, but..." Eve didn't have a chance to protest.

"I'm not asking you to do this right away, but the next time you're in her house, I wish you would take a look around and see if you can spot the vase anywhere. You don't have to open any drawers. Just casually glance around. She won't think that you're looking for it. This is why I wanted to talk to you tonight. I was afraid Pearl would see me coming over here during the day. She might suspect something."

"Couldn't you ask her yourself? There must be something you could say, something that wouldn't be too embarrassing..." Eve was searching frantically for an excuse to avoid dealing with her neighbor's request.

"I don't think I could bring myself to talk to that woman again about anything...and certainly not about my vase. No, I don't even want to go into her house. There's no telling what she's capable of doing. If she's stolen from me, I wonder what else she could do...or what she's already done, for that matter."

Abruptly, Maggie pushed herself up from the chair. "Help me, Eve. You're the only one I trust. Tell Pearl to return my vase. You can tell her that if she puts it by my door, I won't say a word. We'll just pretend she borrowed it. Once I get my vase back, I promise I won't ever say a word about the matter again." The woman stopped talking and cleared her throat.

"Well, I'm not sure I can be of any real help, but I'll see if there's something I can do," Eve replied reluctantly. She remained seated as her neighbor began pacing.

"Thank you. I just knew I could count on you." Abruptly, Maggie turned and darted towards the front door. "Please don't tell anyone else about this...it's too awful," she begged, with her back to Eve.

"No, I won't say a word to anyone. I promise." It was a promise Eve was certain she could easily keep.

"Now, go to bed. I've taken enough of your time for one night," commanded Maggie.

Eve rose slowly, but the woman was already out the door. She stood motionless, stunned by the encounter and what she'd just been asked to do.

When Adam reentered the living room a few minutes later, carrying a tray of cookies, he was surprised to see his wife standing alone in the middle of the room.

"What was that all about?" he asked casually.

"She's very upset. You should have heard her. She thinks Pearl Thomas stole a vase from her house when she was out of town."

"Is that all?" Adam asked, smiling. "Maybe a little paranoid?"

"You have no idea. She was practically on the verge of hysteria and she wants me to go over to Pearl's house and look for her vase. Oh, Adam, I hate to say it, but I think I'm starting to have some doubts about this place. On the surface, everything looks so serene, so orderly and peaceful. But, I wonder what actually goes on behind these stucco walls. I'm afraid that people don't get to live a long time without bringing a few secrets with them and some of these secrets may not be very nice."

"Yes, you may be right. There are probably a good many stories that could be told."

"Mmhm...That's what I'm afraid of, and I really don't think I want to hear them," replied Eve.

Adam took his wife by the elbow and she allowed herself to be led back into the cozy warmth of the bedroom. Somewhere in the distance, the whistling of a siren cut through the silent night.

Chapter 2

When married couples retire, they frequently find themselves forced to spend more time together than usual and, as a result, they may become peevish and irritable with one another. Even the most harmonious relationships can turn bitter in their later years. For Olive and Frank Howell, it didn't take very long for the harshness of this reality to set in. However, it was generally Olive who gave voice to her dissatisfaction and, much to Frank's dismay, this was a frequent occurrence.

They were an oddly matched couple and people who knew them often wondered what possible attraction they might have held for each other at one time. Olive was tall and thin and had dull gray hair that she pulled back into a small, hard knot. Neither her cold, steely eyes nor her tightly drawn lips revealed the slightest hint of a smile. Frank was plump and much shorter than his wife. With his curly-white hair and bushy eyebrows, he looked more like Santa Claus than a beleaguered husband. Their dissimilar outward appearance was also reflected in their different personalities. Unlike his wife, who had no difficulty complaining about every little thing that annoyed her, Frank was mild mannered and rarely expressed displeasure with anything or anybody.

While Olive had no problem with her tongue, she was considerably more uncertain about her legs. Because of the difficulty she experienced walking, she was unable to participate in the many activities that other retired couples had the opportunity to enjoy. The most that Olive was capable of doing was making the short walk to the pool to go for a quick swim and a dip in the Jacuzzi. And this she did religiously, every day, even on the coldest mornings.

What Olive lacked in physical prowess, she made up for in her heightened awareness of everything that went on around her. She kept a close watch on everybody in Sunshine Valley, including Frank. For him, the ability to get away occasionally and play golf during the day provided a sense of peace that he felt he desperately needed if their marriage was to last. However, although Olive didn't overtly forbid him to play, he still paid a price for this short-lived freedom when he returned home.

On most days, Frank would leave the house early in the morning and try to prolong his outing as much as possible. He would play a few rounds, practice his swing, then just sit back in one of the lounge chairs that were lined up by the clubhouse and watch the other players. By evening, as he slowly drove back home, his wife would be waiting for him as she impatiently paced back and forth throughout the house, constantly looking at the clock. He barely had a chance to open the front door when she would erupt into an emotionally charged tirade, hurling endless insults and accusations at him. Such was the routine and this evening was no different, perhaps even a bit worse.

As soon as Frank entered the house, Olive ran at him and started her harangue. He didn't even have time to put away his golf clubs before she began yelling at him. "So, you finally decided to come home...It's okay for you to go out all day and have fun while I have to stay here alone. You're healthy. You're able to walk. You have no idea what it feels like to have my pains." On and on she went. For what seemed like an eternity,

Olive screamed and shouted clichés about her husband's selfishness and thoughtlessness.

For a while, Frank stood silent and listened patiently to his wife's complaints. When she paused for a moment, he turned and slowly made his way into the kitchen. But, Olive wasn't finished. She followed closely behind her husband, resuming her tirade. Once in the kitchen, Frank just stood in the middle of the room, silent and expressionless, as if paralyzed by the sting of his wife's insults. Unrelenting, she continued to lash out at him. The tip of her sharp nose reddened, as it did whenever she became upset, which happened on a daily basis. Slowly, the red flush spread like a web across the rest of her face.

She's winding down now, thought Frank. *In another five minutes it will all be over.* He felt he knew the pattern all too well. The mounting hysteria would reach its peak when Olive started to complain about her pains, then subside, as she began criticizing her surroundings and any or all of the residents of Sunshine Valley.

"You have no understanding," Olive persisted, making sharp clanging noises as she stirred a cloudy mixture of Metamucil and hot water. "I hope you never have to suffer the way I do. You have no idea what it's like. Nobody should have to suffer this much." She swallowed in large gulps, squinting as the thick liquid disappeared slowly down her long thin neck.

Frank and Olive had been married for a little over five years. They met when Frank worked as a waiter in a restaurant in Sunshine Valley. At first, Olive would come in once or twice a week, then, as she and Frank became friendlier, her appearance became a daily ritual. After several months, Frank asked Olive if he could take her out on a real date. It didn't take long before he also proposed marriage, to which she immediately agreed. Soon after they married, Olive insisted that

Frank quit his job. She maintained that she had enough money for the two of them to live comfortably and she didn't want her husband working in such a menial job as having to wait on people.

Frank was drawn to Olive's spunk, as he called it. Even though he knew he didn't really love her, he thought she would make a good companion and that they could have fun together. For Frank, the question of love never even entered the picture. He knew he would never again experience the feelings he felt for his first wife and, of course, his daughter. Whenever he mentioned either of these women, Olive's poorly controlled jealousy would burst into a stream of sarcasm. Once they were married, she began to question Frank unrelentingly, forcing him to make comparisons. Gradually, she grew tired of his attempts to be tactful and would fly into a rage if he even hinted that he had been married before or that he had a daughter to prove it. Although Olive had also been married before, she had no children of her own. Once she found Frank, she wanted to be the sole object of his admiration and attention. She wouldn't admit it, but what she desired most was to be cherished and adored. Her actions and words, however, had the opposite effect. As time passed and Olive's faultfinding increased, Frank withdrew more and more, trying his best to avoid conflict. But, his retreat only served to fuel his wife's discontent.

"I hate it here," continued Olive. "I hate the wind. I hate the quiet. I hate the weather. I hate the Spanish street names I can't pronounce. And, I must say, I don't think the people are very nice here either. They're certainly not nice to me. They could care less if I live or die." A litany of complaints poured out of her tightly pursed lips.

In an attempt to pacify his wife, Frank turned to her and said in a soft voice, "Don't be upset, Olive. I have an idea...Let's go out to dinner tomorrow. We haven't done that in a long time and you always enjoy it. You won't have to cook and I think you'll feel better. We can have chimichangas."

"I don't like chimichangas," she said petulantly. "I want American food. You should know by now I don't like Mexican food."

"Whatever you want," sighed Frank, "We'll go out for American food. I know a nice place that I'm sure you will enjoy."

As the Metamucil began to take effect, the slow internal rumbling gradually gained momentum and forced its way out of Olive's mouth into a loud, sonorous belch. The deep resonance of the sound contrasted curiously with her frail physique. "I think I'll go for an early swim tomorrow. It smells so nice and fresh in the morning." Olive was starting to feel better and even began to caress Frank's hair. Her face showed traces of uncertainty, as if she was confused by her own ranting.

Frank looked up at his wife and thought she appeared a little sad in her thin nightgown, almost vulnerable. "Whatever you want," was all he could manage to say.

In the beginning of their relationship, Frank tried to be empathetic to Olive whenever she started to complain about something. He rationalized that her pains probably accounted for her unpleasant disposition. Nevertheless, although he tried to make her life a little easier, it seemed that she was determined not to let him. Usually, he managed to avoid thinking about his wife's faults. Whenever his thoughts lingered too long on her shortcomings, he would force himself to focus on something more positive. Actually, there were times when Frank even thought himself fortunate. He had a home and someone to cook for him. At other times, however, he felt sorry for himself, lonely and trapped, with no one to talk to or who understood him. Then, he would look around at his surroundings, content with the fact that he was healthy and didn't have to worry about money as did many others who lived in Sunshine Valley. His happiest moments with Olive came when she would prepare his favorite meal of pot roast, mashed potatoes, and apple pie. After such a satisfying dinner, he would pat his round stomach and smile tenderly at the woman with whom he had chosen to spend the rest of his life.

"Now, let's plan where we're going to eat." Olive walked over to her husband and put her long thin arms around his shoulders.

She almost sounds coquettish, thought Frank. "It's a surprise," he responded. "You'll find out tomorrow and I think you're gonna love it."

"Well," snapped Olive, exasperated with Frank's feeble attempts to placate her, "if you're going to be like that, we might as well go to bed. We can skip dinner tonight. I know you've already eaten and so have I." She turned abruptly and headed for the bedroom, expecting her obedient husband to follow her lead.

Reluctantly, Frank shuffled down the hallway, right behind his wife, knowing full well that, like the days, even the nights were under her control. If, for example, he would awaken and need to use the bathroom, he tried to hold off as long as possible until he thought Olive was asleep, then he would sneak out of bed and tiptoe across the dark room. Invariably, however, she would call out after him, "Turn on the light so you can see what you're doing, and don't forget to flush the toilet when you're finished." If he took too long, she would scream out. "What are you doing in there,

Frank? Are you eating again? You know it's not good
for you to eat in the middle of the night...especially the
junk food you eat." Olive was on guard night and day.
Ever vigilant, there was little she did not notice.

The Howells slept in separate beds in a large master
bedroom at the rear of the one-story stucco house. As
was their custom, Olive undressed first, while Frank sat
on the edge of his bed and set the alarm clock. It took
about thirty minutes for her to perform the nightly
ritual. First, she would remove her false teeth, rinse
them, then carefully place them in the container labeled
"Mother." After wiping her face with a damp
washcloth, she would slip into her over-sized pink
flannel nightgown, lubricate her hands and arms, then
walk over to her husband to say "good night." She
always spoke in a firm tone, as if declaring that the day
had officially come to an end. Frank would smile at her,
then be forced to inhale the scent of rose glycerin as she
gave him a quick peck on the cheek.

This evening, as she pulled back the heavy blanket,
propped up her two pillows, and eased herself into bed,
Olive heaved a deep sigh of contentment. Usually, her
face would be beaming with a smug look of self-
righteousness or it would be tense with suspicion. Now,
she seemed almost relaxed. Her thin lips even seemed
to reveal the hint of a rare smile.

Frank set the alarm for seven, pleased with the
knowledge that, for a few hours at least, he would be
able to escape from the sound of his wife's shrill voice
and have some peace. He walked over to the large
sliding door that opened on to the patio and looked out.
Noticing the lights on at the Iversons' house, he
wondered how much of Olive's performance they had
heard. He knew they could hear her, but was grateful
that Adam had never mentioned anything to him about
the nightly tirades. Frank pulled the door shut, locked it,

then drew the heavy drapes and slowly turned to face his wife.

"Tomorrow is going to be a very interesting day," said Olive as she began humming to herself. "Are you planning on playing golf again?" She looked up at Frank without a trace of her usual anger.

"If the weather's nice...I thought I might play a few holes," stammered Frank.

"I suspected as much. You seem to be playing more than ever these days. Oh well," she said dismissing him, "You go ahead. I've got my own agenda. I'm going to have some fun myself. Yes, indeed, it's my turn to have a little fun in this dreary town."

Olive paused for a moment and waited for Frank to ask what she had on her mind, but he had learned better and hoped the lack of interest would quiet her down. "As ye sow, so shall ye reap," she said sanctimoniously, then picked up the Bible from the nightstand and began turning the pages.

As unpleasant as Frank found Olive's harangues, he hated her self-righteousness even more and tried to change the subject. "Where did this fruit come from?" he asked, pointing to a basket full of apples that stood on the floor. He thought it seemed oddly out of place in the otherwise tidy room.

"Dave Wilcox brought it. He stopped by the house this afternoon. He said he had some extra baskets and thought we might enjoy the apples. I put it there for you since you always seem to get so hungry during the night. Apples are good for you. Sure better than the candy you're always sucking on."

But, Olive was not interested in discussing the benefits of fruit and continued her own line of thinking. "We've lived here almost five years now and you know what?" She didn't allow Frank to respond. "I know more about what's going on here than most people and some of it isn't at all good, or even legal, for that matter. So, since nobody else is going to do it, I intend to set a few things straight. You don't care either, do you?" she asked, glaring at her husband. "You don't care if there are criminals living here."

She's starting up again, thought Frank, as he pulled back the covers on his bed. This wasn't like her. Once she got into bed, Olive would usually read a few pages from the Bible, for inspiration and comfort she claimed, then fall into something resembling sleep.

"Do you?" Olive persisted.

"Do I what?" Frank asked, reluctantly.

"You don't care that some folks aren't what they seem to be and that they even break the law when they feel like it."

"I don't know what you're talking about," Frank responded.

"No, of course you don't. All you think about is yourself and having fun. You believe anything people tell you. They'd take advantage of you right and left if it weren't for me watching out for you." Olive was determined to continue talking. "Especially those two women who call themselves sisters."

"Doty and Paula?" asked Frank. "They're nice ladies. They don't take advantage of me. They just like to have someone to talk to." Frank's voice was barely audible.

"Hah!" she exclaimed, pleased that he had taken the bait. "That goes to show you! I'm well aware of what you're up to. Running over to their house whenever you can. You tell me you're going for a walk, but don't think I don't know that you head straight for those two women. It's quite obvious when you've been to their house. I can tell by the look on your face. Like you're so special. I'll bet they say all kinds of things to turn your head and, you know what gets me?"

"What's that?" Frank asked reluctantly, not really wanting to hear any more. *But,* he thought, *he better seem interested or things would get worse.*

"You fall for it too. You fall for all that sweet talk about Frank can do this and Frank is good at that. It's pretty obvious what they're all about." She pushed herself upright, swaying the upper half of her body mockingly. "Pretty soon, before you even realize it, you're in their closet, putting up shelves or fixing a door knob. Now, tell me am I not right?"

"I don't do that much," responded Frank, even though he knew it was useless to protest. He hated it when Olive criticized Doty and Paula. They were the only two other women in Sunshine Valley with whom he would spend time. He was very fond of both of them and enjoyed being in their company. They could laugh together and he loved the fact that they had a piano. He found special pleasure in playing it while Doty would sit beside him and sing.

"Don't try to fool me...I know what you're up to. And don't give me that business about how nice it is for two sisters to get along so well. They call themselves sisters...Hah! Knowing you, I'm sure you believe everything they tell you, but you can't fool me. I've been around too long and seen too much."

"I don't know what you're talking about," said Frank.

"You'll see," Olive responded mysteriously. "But," she added, quickly changing the object of her attack, "they aren't the only ones, and by no means, the worst. Believe me, I intend to set a few things straight. But, first things first. I want to deal with that so-called gardener, Raul, when I see him. I have a few things I'd like to settle with him."

"I hope you're not going to cause any trouble." As soon as he uttered the words, Frank regretted his remark. He knew he should just let things subside, but he had rarely seen his wife in such a spiteful mood. She was generally difficult to get along with, he knew that, but he'd not seen her this overwrought in a long time.

"Trouble? You think I'm the one who starts everything? You think it's my fault that people are so dishonest, that they come here illegally and take jobs from Americans?" Her toothless mouth made the high-pitched words sound like hissing. "The law is the law. I didn't make it up. And, let me tell you, you're very lucky to have me. I know you don't appreciate it, but you will when I'm gone. If more people were like me, this would be a better world. If more people obeyed the law and read the Bible, there would be a lot less grief in the world. Of that, you can be sure."

Frank didn't fully understand why Olive was so overwrought, but realized that, unlike most other evenings, tonight's storm was not going to end soon. He began pacing back and forth, agitated by his wife's continued threats, then picked up the basket of apples and carried them out of the room.

"Are you going to eat again," whined Olive.

"No...I just want to put the apples in the kitchen and I thought I'd give a little something to Petticoat." Despite his frustration, Frank managed to sound calm.

"Be sure she eats it and don't forget to clean her bowl when she's finished. I hate it when cat food sits out all night."

Frank's daughter had given him a cat, thinking the pet would be a good diversion for him. "If you get tired of Olive," she told him teasingly, "you can always run after Petticoat and she won't get mad at you."

The Siamese was lying curled up on a chair in the living room. Reluctantly, Olive allowed Frank to keep the animal, but he had to promise to assume full responsibility for its care. Frank agreed to all of his wife's demands and kept a separate cabinet where he stored the cat's food, toys, and litter. It was the one place Olive never looked. It was also the one place where Frank could hoard little treasures for himself— candy, a cigar or two, even a small bottle of Canadian Club. As he opened the cabinet and took out some dry food for Petticoat, he also helped himself to a chocolate covered cherry. Olive hated it when he ate candy. She hated it when he ate anything she had not prescribed for him. Rather than argue with his wife, Frank maintained his own personal arsenal of forbidden fruit and helped himself whenever he felt the urge to snack.

"Come here, Petticoat. I've got something for you." The large gray cat sauntered into the kitchen, blinking her sleepy eyes, curious to see what was being offered. She sniffed at the food, then looked back at Frank as if to ask, "Is this what you got me up for?" After a few seconds, she returned to her warm hollow.

"I don't blame you," said Frank. He picked up the bowl and poured the food back into the box, swallowed his candy, then reluctantly returned to the battlefield.

Olive was involved in her reading and didn't look up when her husband entered the room. Pulling back the covers, Frank slid into his bed and rolled over, turning his back to his wife. *Surely,* he thought, *she doesn't have anything more to say or complain about.* But, after a few minutes, she started humming.

"How much do you think we could get for this house?" Olive asked abruptly.

Now, what? Frank wasn't sure how much more he could endure. "I don't know," he mumbled. Since Olive had paid for the house and the title was in her name, he never gave much thought to the price or whether they should sell it or not. He actually liked the house and hoped they could continue living there.

"Dave Wilcox said home prices are going up. He thinks we could make a nice profit. If we decided to sell. I wonder...Oh well, I'll deal with him tomorrow too."

Without saying another word, Olive snapped her Bible shut, leaned over, and turned out the light on the night stand that separated the two beds.

- - - - -

Doty O'Brian and Paula McGuire, or, the Irish sisters, as everyone referred to them, were among the first of the new pioneers to settle in Sunshine Valley. Originally from Milwaukee, they found life in Arizona much to their liking. Paula was the first to retire and, shortly after she quit working, she began to investigate several communities in the Midwest, but found nothing that appealed to her. Because she didn't particularly like the idea of living in such cold weather the rest of her life, when some friends told her about Sunshine Valley, she flew to Tucson, rented a car, and made the twenty-five mile trip south to inspect the small town.

Although she found the desert beautiful, all that Paula saw as she drove down the highway were stretches of barren prairie and an isolated ranchito that dotted the landscape here and there. *It certainly doesn't look like many people live around here*, she thought. After driving for thirty minutes, she made a right turn onto the main road that led into Sunshine Valley. What a surprise and what a difference! As she drove through the town, she passed numerous beige and white stucco homes that were beautifully landscaped. She even spotted a few shopping malls with stores, restaurants, and art galleries. Like so many others before her, Paula immediately fell in love with what she saw and it didn't take her long to find a house that she liked. After two days of carefully inspecting the different models that were for sale, she settled on a two-bedroom plan in

Vista Verde Estates and made a down payment. Full of excitement, she returned to Milwaukee to share the good news with Doty. They immediately gave notice on the apartment they were renting, then, six months later, both women packed their bags and headed for their little gem in the desert. Now, after seven years, they never once regretted their decision.

Paula had been a seamstress for more than forty years. She enjoyed the peace and quiet of not having to interact with other people. Doty, the more gregarious of the pair, found her place as a concierge in a small boutique hotel. Unlike Paula, she loved meeting and talking with people and helping them find their way around the city. Despite having worked all their adult lives, neither of the women received a pension, so, in the years that followed their retirement, they were forced to lived frugally, denying themselves small pleasures such as going to movies or eating out in a restaurant. Together with personal savings and Social Security, they managed to live a limited, but comfortable life. The one luxury they afforded themselves was a grand piano and this, they both acknowledged, was a basic necessity, one they could not live without.

Paula and Doty were not actually related to each other, but most people assumed they were sisters. They hadn't consciously set out to deceive anyone, but, when they moved to Sunshine Valley, for some reason, the neighbors thought they were sisters and the women saw no reason to correct the mistake. After a while, it seemed awkward to have to clarify the misunderstanding and, as they often said to each other, since they had lived together for over thirty years and knew each other so well, they actually felt like sisters. At the pool, people often commented on the similarities between the two women and so, the private joke was perpetuated.

"Are those coyotes I hear?" Doty asked Paula who had just put some music on the phonograph.

"I don't hear anything," replied Paula, humming the familiar strains of *The Marriage of Figaro*, not recognizing that she was playing a recording of *The Barber of Seville.*

"Turn the sound down a minute," Doty said in a loud voice.

Paula did as she was told, then said, "I still don't hear anything." She tilted her head back and carefully brushed a wisp of gray hair to one side.

But, Doty heard the howling and realized immediately that it wasn't the sound of coyotes that permeated the desert silence. Even through the closed doors, she recognized the high-pitched wailing of Olive Howell. "It's that shrew," she informed Paula and, without missing a beat, added, "Poor Frank. She's screaming at him again."

Paula strained to hear the shouting. "If she's not talking his ear off quoting the Scriptures, then she's yelling at him for something he's done or hasn't done."

"Yes, poor Frank. He's such a nice man," sighed Doty. "He deserves better. I don't know how he can put up with her. I'm really surprised he hasn't left her."

"Yes," agreed Paula. "He's quite decent, but everyone has a limit. Olive is not a very happy person and she certainly lets everyone know it. I think someone should take her out into the desert and just put an end to her misery. She's a despicable woman."

Doty concurred. They both enjoyed Frank's company. Having run into him on numerous occasions while they were out walking, Paula and Doty eventually befriended the seemingly shy man. At first, they started doing little things for him. They would invite him into the house for a cool drink on hot afternoons and give him magazines and newspapers. Frank repaid their generosity by offering to repair a broken door spring or a leaky faucet. His eyes lit up one day when he noticed their piano. In his slow, soft speech, he told them how he used to play in a band when he was younger. The piano brought them all closer. Frank would play songs they all knew, while Doty, who still had a good voice, would sit beside him on the bench and sing.

"Anyway," continued Paula, "a person can't go around making life unpleasant for everyone else without suffering the consequences. Mark my words. I've seen it before. This woman is going to come to a bad end."

"What do you mean?" asked Doty cautiously.

"Miserable people like that usually don't have happy endings. You remember my Aunt Mae, don't you?"

"Oh, yes, I'd forgotten all about her. I only met her once. They never found her body, did they?"

"Nope...just her car...way out in the woods...nowhere near her home. Nobody knows what happened to her. She was a pistol, that one, lots of enemies, just like Olive, and someone finally put an end to it all."

"I hate to wish bad things on a person, but maybe one of these days Olive will have an accident, if you catch my drift. It would be good for Frank if something did happen to her and she was out of his life...forever."

"And it would be good for us too...and, I might add, all of Sunshine Valley, for that matter. She doesn't belong here. It would be a real blessing for everyone if she just disappeared."

"Well," said Doty, pushing herself up from her chair, "Enough of this. I'm going to bed. I want to get an early start tomorrow. Are you coming?"

"No, I think I'll sit here for a while and listen to some nice music. I'm not really very tired and music soothes my nerves. No use tossing and turning for an hour."

"I know," added Doty. "That's why I took a Valium."

"You really seem to be going through those pills in a hurry," added Paula.

"Me?" Doty sounded surprised.

"Who else? I noticed that the bottle is almost empty."

"Yes, it is, but I just assumed you were taking them," Doty countered.

"I do take one now and then, but it seems like we're running out sooner than usual. I think we should try to be a bit more careful."

"Well, yes," Doty added hesitantly. "You're probably right. Perhaps we should both go back to warm milk."

"Don't be silly," replied Paula, patting her hair as she always did when she felt ill at ease. "I can always ask the gardener Raul to get a refill when he goes back to Mexico. He helps a lot of folks here with their medications and he doesn't seem to mind. And, besides, they're less expensive in Mexico. Now, go to bed and let me enjoy this music for awhile."

"Have you seen those old issues of *Time* that I was saving?" Doty asked, searching the stack of magazines piled up on the floor.

"Time? What did you say about the time?" Paula looked at her watch and replied, "Ten thirty."

Paula was what other women referred to as plain. She wore no makeup and, although she was clean, she paid little attention to her appearance. When she smiled, however, as she did now, her expression was warm and pleasant.

"Thank you," replied Doty. It disturbed her that Paula's hearing appeared to be failing so rapidly. She had urged her friend to get a hearing aid, but the older woman was very proud and stubbornly refused to acknowledge any physical impairment. So, Doty took upon herself the burden of Paula's deteriorating hearing by speaking louder and more slowly and overlooking any mistakes her companion would make. More than anything, she wanted to help maintain Paula's self-confidence. She went along with her pretense of stubbornness, but knew that the real reason Paula resisted getting a hearing aid was the expense. Doty wished she could find the money somewhere and give it to Paula. But, she knew the budget was tight and didn't allow for extra purchases, especially for something as expensive as a hearing aid.

"Make sure everything is turned off before you come to bed," Doty said to her companion, as she prepared to leave the room.

"Yes, of course, but later. I won't be too long. I just want to sit here for a while and let my mind wander a bit."

Doty left Paula to her own pleasures. She paused briefly in the kitchen when she noticed the pork chops and sauerkraut they had eaten for dinner were still sitting on the counter. *Oh, dear*, she thought, *I forgot to put this away.* She sniffed the plate, then carefully wrapped the food and put it in the refrigerator. Doty did most of the shopping and cooking and she prided herself on how well she was able to manage the seventy-five dollars a week she and Paula allowed themselves for food. With the help of coupons, sales, and special reductions on day-old bakery goods, she thought they fared quite well. She often wished they could have dinner parties, but she knew this was impossible. Maybe if we win the lottery, she would say jokingly.

"Good night," Doty called to her friend, not expecting a response.

As she made her way into the bedroom, she could still hear Olive shouting at Frank. *Aunt Mae,* she reflected and shook her head. *Too bad Olive doesn't drive a car.*

Chapter 3

The following morning, the alarm clock next to Frank's bed began ringing at six thirty, as it did every morning. Groping in the semi-darkness, he leaned over and switched the button to "Off." After a few minutes, he pushed his feet from under the warm covers, rolled out of bed and stepped into the fur-lined slippers that were waiting for him on the floor. Not yet ready to face the day, Olive groaned and pulled the blanket up over her shoulders. As was her custom, she would wait for her husband to make coffee before joining him in the kitchen.

Flinging on his red and blue plaid robe, Frank headed for the living room to turn up the thermostat and pull back the heavy green drapes to let in some early morning light. The cold air made hissing and crackling noises as it rushed through the Juniper trees. He stood by the window for a moment, watching the triangular leaves of the vines that grew along the patio wall tremble in the wind. Raising his shoulders, Frank cupped his hands and blew into them, then turned to go into the kitchen. On his way, he stopped to pet his cat who was curled up in her cozy nest. She opened one drowsy eye and looked up. "Come on, Coats. I'll fix you some breakfast." She turned over on her back, stretched and yawned, then slowly raised herself and followed her master as he made his way into the kitchen.

Meanwhile, Olive inched her way out of bed and stumbled into the bathroom. Because it would take a while for the heat to warm the house, she began to shiver as she performed her morning ablutions. First the teeth. She rinsed them thoroughly, then popped them into her sunken mouth. As she washed her face, she beamed with pride at the reflection in the mirror. *I certainly am a clean woman,* she thought. On that point, everyone who knew her had to agree. What they didn't know was that, having turned off the hot water in her own house to save money, she managed to stay clean by taking hot showers when she went to the pool. It wasn't so much a question of not having sufficient income. Actually, Olive Howell was probably one of the wealthiest women in Sunshine Valley. But, by turning off the hot water, she prided herself on being able to save, according to her calculations, more than two hundred dollars a year. Besides finding ways to save money, the one other activity that gave Olive personal pleasure was keeping a tidy house. She would float through each room on a daily basis, dusting every piece of furniture, whether it was needed or not. Cleanliness and frugality were two virtues she admired and she was proud of the way she'd managed to achieve both.

Frank's back was turned as Olive crept into the kitchen and began looking around. "Be sure to tidy up the mess you make before leaving the house. And another thing," she said, as she craned her neck and sniffed the air, "it's starting to stink in here. I wish you could keep that animal outside. She's not very clean and she makes the house smell like a zoo. You know how I hate bad smells, especially in my own home. I try to keep things nice and clean and then you have to go and undue all my hard work."

Frank was standing by his private cabinet, making scraping sounds as he spooned the cat food into a dish. The Siamese, arching her back high in the air, brushed against his legs. "Petticoat isn't dirty...she's very clean," he protested feebly, then placed the dish on the floor. The cat smacked her lips as she eagerly lapped up the food.

"Here's your coffee," Frank continued, as he handed a cup to Olive who'd propped herself up in a chair at the table. "It's hot. I just poured it...and I already put sugar in it...exactly the way you like it."

"Not too much, I hope. You've been putting too much sugar in my coffee lately. It's not good to eat too much sugar, you know."

Frank ignored the comment and sat down at the table to eat a breakfast that consisted of two pieces of toast with strawberry jam, a glass of orange juice, and a cup of black coffee. He chewed slowly and deliberately. Olive didn't join him, preferring to avoid any food until lunch time. Although he was anxious to leave the house, he knew that Olive was well aware of his eagerness, so he deliberately took small bites and chewed longer than necessary to avoid providing fuel for another outburst. But, to Frank's surprise, this morning, unlike the previous evening, his wife didn't seem to pay much attention to him.

"I feel really good today," she said, as she swallowed the last drop of coffee. "It's going to be interesting to see what happens. I have such big plans."

Frank knew better than to ask Olive any questions and just kept eating.

After wiping some imaginary crumbs from the corners of her mouth, Olive began to rock back and forth in her chair. Finally, she slapped her knee and said, "Well, that's it. I'm off. Now, don't forget, you promised to take me out to dinner tonight. You know I like to eat early, so don't stay out all day like you usually do. I don't know how you can play golf in this wind anyway. Be sure to lock the door when you leave and don't forget your sunglasses." A list of instructions tripped off her tight lips.

Olive walked from room to room, stopping occasionally to look with pride at all the objects she'd managed to collect over the years. She was especially fond of the porcelain hand-painted birds sitting on the shelf that lined the dining room wall. They'd been a gift from her first husband, a souvenir of happier times she often thought to herself.

As Olive made her way through the house, she left behind a trail of lemon-scented air freshener. A clever touch, she smiled knowingly to herself. By spraying the fragrance in the air, she could always tell if Frank had eaten, or, even worse, smoked something he wasn't supposed to when she wasn't watching. Following her usual routine, she wiped an imaginary speck of dust from a lamp and patted the hand-crocheted pillows that were propped up on the couch that nobody was allowed to sit on. She opened the front closet and took out the shopping bag that contained her swimming paraphernalia. After checking to make certain everything was in place—towel, slippers, Vaseline, bathing cap—she put on a brown wool robe, pulled a clear plastic hood snugly over her head, then exited through the patio.

As Olive headed down the empty street towards the pool, she walked at an unusually brisk pace, considering her arthritis. She tightened the belt of her robe and sucked in her cheeks. On this cold, windy morning, she seemed to be enjoying a heady sense of power. Filled with exuberance, she started to sing, softly at first, then louder and bolder, stirred by the words. "Rescue the perishing, pray for the dying. Save them in pity o'er all the earth." Louder and louder, her voice resonated through the quiet street.

Doors opened and slammed shut as Olive made her way past the houses. A dog began barking somewhere in the distance. She stopped occasionally to peer into a patio. Her mind was racing. With growing confidence, she thought about the mission she'd set for herself. "Blessed are they who hunger and thirst after righteousness," she whispered as she continued marching.

Lifting her head against the wind, Olive arrived at the pool and spotted the mailman, Tom Wicks, who'd stopped across the street in front of the house with the "For Sale" sign in the window. He was talking to the realtor, Dave Wilcox, who was sitting in his car, evidently waiting to show the house to a prospective buyer.

"Say, Tom, have you seen the gardener Raul anywhere this morning?" Olive's sharp voice cut through the morning air like a knife as she screamed to the mailman.

"No", the man replied, shaking his head. "I haven't seen him today."

"If you do run into him, tell him to come over to my house. I want to speak to him."

"Will do. I'll let him know you're looking for him."

As usual, Olive had difficulty breathing after her long walk and began to cough. She hesitated a few seconds, then unlocked the gate and entered the pool area, where she noticed some branches and twigs that were swept into a pile. A couple of shovels and a rake were lying on the ground. She looked around, but didn't see the man who owned the tools. *It's too early for his siesta,* she thought. Peering around the corner of the building that housed the dressing room, she noticed Doty O'Brian and Paula McGuire. Paula was stuffing something into her bag as Doty emerged from the dressing room. Both women stopped what they were doing and looked over at Olive, but neither of them said a word.

"Good morning, girls," chirped Olive, glad the two women were getting ready to leave. She'd have the pool to herself and could take a leisurely shower without having to engage in conversation with anyone.

Paula packed the remainder of their belongings, while Doty wrapped a towel around her damp hair. "Here...put this around your neck," Paula said to her younger companion and handed her a flowered scarf. "You'll need it. It's really cold this morning." Doty did as she was told.

"Did you wash your hair in there?" snapped Olive. "You know it's against the rules to wash your hair in the shower. You could be banned from coming here in the future if you don't obey the rules."

Neither of the women said a word. They felt it was unnecessary to defend their behavior. They simply ignored Olive and quickly made their way through the gate and out onto the street.

At ten o'clock, Eve and Adam packed their small plastic bags, then left the house and started for the pool. Once outside, however, they stopped for a moment and looked at each other questioningly. Given the chill in the air, they wondered if it was such a good idea to go to the pool so early. Although Eve began to shiver and regretted that she hadn't worn something warmer, they decided to continue walking, only a little faster. The blue cloudless sky and the bright sunlight made the square stucco houses look like blocks of ice. After two weeks of sharp frost, the plants in the front yards had frayed and were starting to wither. Here and there, an American flag waved in the breeze.

As they walked towards the pool, they spotted Tom Wicks who was starting to fill a mailbox. "Morning," he greeted the couple. "Kind of chilly for a swim, isn't it?"

"We're going to the pool to thaw out," replied Adam. "The water's usually much warmer than the air...and the Jacuzzi's even hotter. At least the sun is out today."

Tom smiled and continued filling the box as Eve and Adam made their way to the pool. Across the street, Eve noticed their neighbor Pearl Thomas who was busy pulling up weeds in her front garden. She was suddenly reminded of the disturbing conversation she'd had with Maggie Walsh the previous evening. Pearl waved, as friendly as always, and Eve returned the greeting. She found the whole matter of the missing vase very distasteful and had concluded during the night that she would urge Maggie to confront Pearl and resolve the issue herself. It wasn't at all in Eve's nature to sneak around and spy on others and she found it difficult to believe that Pearl was a thief.

The wind had died down and, once again, the familiar desert silence began to settle in around them. The all encompassing stillness made Eve feel like an intruder in a mystical world that gave the illusion of timelessness. She looked at her husband's back and thick white curly hair and felt secure, knowing that he was in such good health. The fact that he was so tall gave her added pleasure and made her feel taller too, she thought, even though she just barely made it to five feet. Although Eve believed she was slightly overweight and had her mind set on losing a few pounds, according to Adam, she was perfect. She had bright blue eyes and short blond hair for which she received many compliments. As she often explained, both her mother and grandmother maintained their blond hair well into their nineties and never used any dye. Since Eve was six months older than Adam, she often found herself using the difference to her advantage whenever they got into a disagreement about an issue. Actually, Adam liked the fact that his wife was older. It made her seem all the more interesting to him.

"What a lovely morning," said Eve, as she inhaled the fresh air. "I feel like I've been reborn. I don't know exactly how to describe it, but I always feel there's something very spiritual about this place."

Indeed, there were times when Sunshine Valley seemed like a veritable paradise. Snatches of prairie were visible between the houses and, in the distance, uniquely shaped cacti jutted up against a stark background of jagged purple mountains. Here and there, a spiny, twisted cholla sprang up, resembling something left over from pre-historic times. The silence became more embracing. Eve felt it throughout her body. At this moment, she had the sensation that very little had changed since the beginning of time. But, even though it couldn't be seen or heard, the landscape was changing, slowly, silently, and imperceptibly, as it had for centuries.

"I still can't get over how lucky we are," Eve said with conviction, as she took Adam's arm. "Each day seems more beautiful than the one before. I just love the landscape and the way people have fixed up the outside of their homes. You can tell they enjoy living here. What really intrigues me are the different types of cactus that grow here. I never knew there were so many varieties."

"The shapes are interesting," said Adam, "and I love the way you paint them too. I don't know which is more beautiful...the real thing or your representation."

Eve turned to her husband and smiled. Because her teaching took up most of her time, she never had the chance to paint when she worked and had been waiting for years to get started. As soon as she moved to Sunshine Valley, she found an art supply store where she bought a box of acrylic paints, several brushes, a pile of different-sized canvases, and a small easel. Once home, she made a comfortable arrangement for herself on the patio and began her artistic career in earnest by painting a series of Saguaro cacti. With the help of Adam, she even managed to get two of them accepted for a show by a local art gallery. Gradually, as she gained more confidence, she expanded her subject matter by capturing the bright colors of the desert in large landscapes.

"I meant to ask you," continued Adam, "have you heard anything from the gallery about your paintings? Do you know if either of them has sold? I'll bet you've made a sale."

"I haven't heard a word yet," replied Eve. "Actually, I was thinking of running over there to see what's happening."

The residents of Vista Verde Estates generally walked to the pool or drove there in a golf cart. On most days, by this time, a row of carts would be lined up along the street in front of the white-washed brick enclosure, but, not this morning. Now and then, a lone figure could be seen jogging, but, due to the recent cold spell, only the hardiest of souls dared to venture out early. Adam and Eve didn't mind. In fact, they preferred it when they had the pool to themselves and could splash around as they wished without having to engage in conversation or worry about disturbing other people.

"I think I'll try for fifteen laps this morning," said Eve. "I've been getting stronger and one of these days I'll make it to thirty again. That's what I used to do in my twenties and that's my goal now...how about you?"

"Well," replied Adam, "I haven't been keeping track, but I think it's wonderful what you're doing. You're a good role model. Maybe I should start counting."

When they arrived at the pool gate, Adam pointed to two empty cars that were parked across the street. "Looks like Dave is showing Harry's place to someone." He and Eve stopped for a moment to look across at the house. A couple emerged from the front door, followed by the realtor. Automatically, as was the local custom, the realtor raised his right arm, white shirt sleeve rolled up to the elbow, and waved to the Iversons. They waved back politely, as was also the custom, then turned to enter the pool, careful to avoid a pile of branches that were scattered on the ground.

Just as they were about to enter the pool area, Alice Webber, another neighbor, came running towards them and called out, "Wait a minute...could you hold the gate?"

"Don't run, Alice," Eve said to the woman. "Take your time. We're in no hurry."

"I forgot my key." The woman was panting.

Adam held the door open for the two women Eve disappeared into the dressing room while her husband went to check the temperature of the water. He knelt down by the shallow end of the pool, then hoisted the long, thin silver cylinder, turned it over in the palm of his hand, and squinted, as he tried to read the small numbers.

"Eighty-seven," he announced.

"That's perfect," shouted Eve from inside the dressing room. As she was putting her bag down on a bench, she looked up and was surprised to see Olive Howell's familiar brown robe hanging on a hook. She thought it odd that the woman who was so meticulous about everything would leave her robe behind, especially on such a cold morning. Eve didn't have time to wonder much longer. All of a sudden, she heard a shrill scream. She opened the dressing room door and ran outside to see what was happening. Alice was leaning over the Jacuzzi, staring motionless, as if paralyzed.

From where she was standing, Eve noticed what appeared to be a bright piece of cloth floating in the steaming, churning water. For a moment, she thought it was a towel that had been blown from a nearby chair. People often forgot their towels, even bathing suits, and it was windy. Forcing herself to move closer, she tried to get a better look. Suddenly, a foot that seemed to come from nowhere propelled itself into the air. Now, there was no doubt about it. Despite the surge of bubbling water, Eve was able to make out the figure of a woman swirling around in the tiny pool.

Adam ran to the Jacuzzi, leaned over the edge and tried to grab an arm of the twisted torso. *Thankfully, all body parts were intact,* he thought, but, due to the turbulence of the water, he was unable to get a firm grip on the woman. After several failed attempts, he yelled, "turn off the motor."

Stunned by the sight of the body, Alice stumbled backwards, quickly turned off the jet stream of water, then braced herself against a cold, metal table. All of a sudden, Eve felt overcome by a rush of nausea. She'd never experienced such a feeling before and it took her by surprise. As Adam worked to pull the body out of the Jacuzzi, the woman seemed to come alive, arms flailing in the air, splashing water on the cement. On top of her stomach, a pink terrycloth slipper bobbed up and down.

Eve and Alice stood frozen in silence as Adam knelt over the body, carefully examining it for bruises or blood.

"It's Olive," he said solemnly. "There's no pulse. She's dead. She must have drowned."

A stream of water belched out of the nostrils and mouth of the lifeless body The bubbles of air that escaped from under her bathing suit made odd popping sounds. Eve gazed somberly at the distorted body and thought she looked like a frail statue that had, due to many years of exposure to all kinds of weather, finally broken off from its pedestal and fallen into the fountain. The irony of the slipper, still intact on her stomach, didn't escape Eve. *Well, how about that*, she thought, *after all this time, Olive is now the one who is 'unter den pantofeln,' and literally so.*

Calmly, but with a voice of authority, Adam issued instructions to the two women. "Eve, would you go and call the sheriff? I think you should go with her Alice. I'll stay here with the body until the authorities arrive...and be sure not to touch anything."

Eve took a deep breath, then locked arms with the other woman, and moved quickly towards the gate. She stopped for a moment and looked back over her shoulder. By the side of the Jacuzzi, in the shade of the evening primrose that formed a ragged border, a horned toad sat breathing deeply, thrusting its tiny chest, in and out, in and out.

Chapter 4

As was to be expected, the main topic of conversation in the days that followed, revolved around the death of Olive Howell. Nothing like this had ever happened in Sunshine Valley before. That is not to say that people didn't die, but when they did, some pool regulars observed, they had the good taste to pass on in the privacy of their own homes or at least in a hospital bed. Some of the long-time residents who knew Olive thought it was just like her, choosing to drown in a public place, thus spoiling it for everyone else.

For five days following the discovery of the body, the pool was closed, as a team of law enforcement officers and forensic specialists set about their investigation. Eve was quite content to avoid the unpleasant scene and took the opportunity to do some painting. With help from Adam, she brought out her paints and several canvases to the patio and set up her easel on the table. "I'm not very eager to go back to the pool for a while," she said as she sat down. "I still have a very clear mental picture of Olive's body floating in the water...not something I particularly want to be reminded of. So, now, I'm going to try to fill my head with more pleasant images."

"I don't blame you," said Adam. "The sight of her lifeless body was really quite a shock...for me too. I'd just as soon avoid the pool myself."

"You know, the light is good here," said Eve, eager to avoid talking about Olive and the discovery of her body. "It helps me paint better. I never realized the importance of good lighting, but, now I do. I think that's why so many artists went to the south of France."

"Well, I sure like what you've been doing, and you're doing it right here in Sunshine Valley," said Adam, as he patted his wife on the shoulder.

"I love painting landscapes—all kinds. I have to remember to take a sketch pad with me when we go to Germany. I know there are some lovely settings there that I sure would love to capture...the Rhine, the Elbe...maybe even the Black Forest."

"That's a great idea. You'll have plenty of opportunity when I'm not around. Right now, I'm going to try to forget what we've been through...for you, painting...for me, stamps. I'll be in the den if you need me." Adam turned and reentered the house.

With Coco stretched out at her feet, Eve sat on the patio for the next few days, content to just keep painting. She loved the sense of immediate gratification she received from capturing the desert-inspired shapes and colors. After completing five new canvases, she decided it was time to stop and take a break.

Once the police finished their investigation, the community Jacuzzi was emptied, scrubbed free of any imaginary traces of death, then replenished with clean, fresh water. On the sixth day, rather than avoiding the pool, both the regulars and those who were just curious came in droves and grabbed the chairs that surrounded the shimmering turquoise rectangle.

With some reluctance, Eve also decided to go to the pool now that it had re-opened. Was it curiosity, she wondered? Or, did she just need a little exercise since she'd been sitting for such long periods these past few days? She preferred to believe the latter. Since Adam was deeply involved with his research, he opted not to accompany her.

Upon arriving at the pool, Eve heard a lot of noise coming from inside and, as she opened the gate, was quite stunned to see so many people. *Perhaps this wasn't such a good idea after all,* she thought, but looked around and finally managed to find an empty chair. Now and then, someone would approach her and ask her to describe how she and Adam had found Olive's body. But, she was in no mood to recall the event and simply said, "Anything worth knowing is in the paper. There's nothing else I can add."

The Sunshine Valley News reported the story in detail and everyone either had a copy or shared one with a neighbor. "Local Woman Drowns in Jacuzzi" read the headline. The article stated that "Olive Howell, a resident of Sunshine Valley for the past five years, was found drowned in a community Jacuzzi on Tuesday. The body was discovered by local residents Adam and Eve Iverson at approximately 10:00 a.m. According to Deputy Sheriff Bud Warner, no contusions or abrasions were found and initial findings indicate that the woman's death was accidental. 'Looks like she took a tranquilizer, passed out in the hot water and simply drowned. I've seen it before.' Traces of Valium were found in the woman's blood, and Deputy Warner warned about the dangers of taking medications and sitting unattended in a hot Jacuzzi. Mrs. Howell is survived by her husband Frank. The couple had no children. No funeral services are currently scheduled."

"One thing's for sure, she got what she deserved," commented one woman, as she finished reading the article.

"I can't believe she ever took tranquilizers. Imagine what she would have been like without them," said another.

The gossip at the pool covered every aspect of Olive and Frank Howell's lives. No topic was considered too personal or too trivial. Talk ranged from a rehashing of Olive's insults and threats to speculation about what Frank was going to do with his new found freedom—and wealth—someone added.

"There were many times when I wanted to wring her neck myself."

"I always wondered what such a nice fellow saw in that dried up bag of venom."

"I'll bet he leaves this place."

"I wouldn't be so sure...I think he's got his eye on one of the Irish sisters."

"Doty maybe, but certainly not Paula."

"They say he's quite a lady's man."

"I wonder how much she left him?"

"He better spend it fast...before the police nab him."

"You think he killed her? I wouldn't blame him, if he did."

"This whole thing is a nightmare."

"I think it's quite thrilling...gives me goose bumps...better than a movie."

Eve couldn't help but overhear the different conversations and conjectures that swirled around her. After about thirty minutes, she realized there would be no swimming today. Finally, she felt that she'd heard enough and decided it was time to leave. Pushing herself out of the chair, she grabbed her bag, and swiftly walked to the gate, trying to avoid any eye contact. She passed the Jacuzzi which, despite all the people who were gathered at the pool, remained curiously empty, then left through the gate, and headed for home.

Olive's untimely death provided hours of entertainment and speculation for the residents of this peaceful valley. Overnight, Frank had become the community's wealthiest and most eligible bachelor, but he was too distraught to take advantage of his new status. He stayed indoors most of the time, leaving the house only when he had to buy groceries. He stopped playing golf and didn't even make his usual visits to Doty and Paula's house. Instead, he remained alone and sat in silence to grieve Olive.

Frank had learned about his wife's death at the golf course, just as he was finishing the ninth hole. When Deputy Warner and Adam went to his house and found no one at home, Adam suggested that Frank was probably playing golf at Sunshine Hills and volunteered to go and see if he could find him to break the news about Olive. Happy to be relieved of this burden, the deputy eagerly accepted Adam's offer and asked him to stop by the station with Frank later in the afternoon when they returned.

Adam took his time as he drove out to the golf course, planning how he was going to break the news about Olive. As he pulled into Sunshine Hills and parked the car, he saw Frank walking across the grass. Adam motioned to him, then led him into the clubhouse and found a quiet spot where he carefully began to explain how he and Eve had found Olive's body in the Jacuzzi. When he finished, Adam wasn't sure at first if Frank had heard him correctly. He showed no reaction and simply stood transfixed, gazing out the window at the rolling green hills. After a few moments of silence, Frank nodded his head, acknowledging that he had indeed heard his friend.

Adam explained that they needed to stop by the sheriff's station because Deputy Warner wanted to ask him a few questions.

"We better get going, then," Frank replied solemnly.

"Why don't you come with me, for now," said Adam. "We can take your clubs with us. After we're finished at the sheriff's station, I can drive you back here and you can pick up your car. I'll follow you home."

Adam took his friend's arm and led him back to the car. Except for a lone motorcycle that roared past them, the drive back to Sunshine Valley was a quiet one. Neither Adam nor Frank uttered a word during the entire trip.

When they arrived at the sheriff's station, Deputy Warner greeted the two men warmly and put his arm around Frank. "I expect Adam has told you what happened. I'm truly sorry for your loss," he said. "If there's anything you want to know, I'll try my best to help you. Then, I hope you don't mind, but I also need to ask you a few questions. It's just routine and it won't take long. I'll be as quick as I can."

"I don't know if I can be of much help, but I'll try my best," said Frank.

After he finished the interrogation, the deputy explained that there would be an autopsy and, once it was completed, Olive's body would be released for burial.

Olive had told Frank she wanted to be cremated if she were to die before him. There was to be no funeral and no fuss. She did not want to have people staring and gawking at her and she certainly didn't want strangers making money from her death. Always planning ahead, one of the first things she did after moving to Arizona was to join the local cremation society. She sent in her check for fifty dollars, but didn't realize at the time that she would be able to take advantage of her membership so quickly.

As he had done so well and so often when she was alive, Frank continued to obey Olive's wishes after her death. It only took a few days for the autopsy to be completed. Olive's death was ruled accidental and Frank gave permission to Deputy Warner for the cremation. There would be no funeral. He was relieved that he would be spared the humiliation of having to face people and accept their forced condolences. He knew that nobody was really sorry to see Olive die and he couldn't bear the thought of having to go along with others' pretense of grief. Whatever loss he felt, he would mourn alone.

One week after Olive's death, Adam invited Frank to come for dinner. "I know it might be hard to believe, but he's very upset and lonely," he explained to Eve. "I think he could do with some company."

"I suppose so," Eve replied in a strained voice.

Adam walked over to the closet and opened the door. It was time for Coco's walk and the dog was jumping up and down, dancing excitedly in circles around him. "Come on, Coco," he said, taking the leash from the hook. "Let's go for a stroll."

Adam led the poodle to the edge of the prairie, then unhooked her leash. He took her bone out of his pocket and threw it about twenty-five feet into a clearing. She darted after the twisted piece of rawhide and brought it back, panting and hesitating, pretending she was going to keep it. Finally, she dropped the wet object at Adam's feet and began barking, urging him to throw it again. He repeated the game with her two more times, then clapped his hands. "Okay, Coco, that's enough for now," he said, then turned and headed back to the house. He was preoccupied with thoughts of Frank and wanted to get home before his neighbor arrived for dinner.

At six o'clock exactly, the doorbell rang. Adam crossed the living room and opened the heavy, hand-carved door.

"I hope I'm not too early. You said six." Frank tried to force a smile.

"Come in. You're right on time. Sit down," said Adam, pointing to a deep armchair in the corner of the living room. "I'll bet you could use a drink...gin and tonic okay?"

"Perfect."

"Hello, Frank," Eve called from the kitchen. "Excuse me if I can't come in right now."

"That's okay," Frank replied, awkwardly.

Eve had never really talked much to their neighbor except to say hello when passing him on the street. He was more Adam's friend. Although she found him pleasant enough, there was something about him that made her feel uneasy. She had always found seemingly shy, retiring people rather irksome, difficult to read and not to be trusted. This man was no exception.

After she finished peeling the vegetables, Eve wiped her hands, then went into the living room. She hesitated a moment in the doorway before entering, eyeing Frank and listening to what he was telling Adam. Although she felt a bit like an eavesdropper, she continued watching the man, looking for some hint that might reveal his true feelings. *You never can tell what shy people are really thinking,* she reflected. This is what bothered her most about the trait.

"Here. I think you can use this," said Adam as he handed a glass to his friend.

Sitting back in the armchair, Frank opened and closed his mouth dryly, every other breath filled with some form of apology. Eve was struck by his resemblance to one of the teachers she'd known at school, not so much in looks as in manner. A nice quiet man, not particularly noteworthy, but honest, everyone agreed. Nobody thought Mr. Dennis had any secrets or anything to hide. Then, one day, it was discovered that this paragon of virtue and modesty had been helping himself to doughnuts in the teachers' lounge without paying for them. When no one was looking, Mr. Dennis would slip a few doughnuts into his briefcase. After he was caught in a trap carefully set by the school principal, Mr. Dennis made a discreet arrangement to reimburse the school for his years of remorseless doughnut thievery. *It was a petty infraction*, but, thought Eve, *exactly the kind of crime a shy person would commit.*

For two hours, during and after dinner, everyone successfully avoided talking about Olive. Adam spoke at length about his stamps and showed Frank the new Zeppelin Air Mail cover he'd recently purchased. He described in detail the research he was doing and the trip to Germany that he and Eve were planning. In her attempt to engage Frank in conversation, she suggested that they all drive to Tucson one day to try out a new golf course.

But, for Frank, thoughts of Olive were inescapable. "I have to go to California for a few days," he said. Slowly and carefully, he explained about some property that Olive owned there and that had to be transferred to his name. He would have to see a lawyer and would probably be gone for at least three days. "If it's not too much to ask, do you think you could feed Petticoat while I'm gone?" he remembered to ask Eve.

"Of course, it's not too much to ask. I'll be glad to help in any way I can. Let me know what and when to feed her. I'll go over there to visit her during the day as well."

Eve watched Frank's eyes well up with tears. "Thank you. All of this has been...too much," he replied as he started to sob.

Generally, Eve was a very compassionate person and would make a great effort to console someone who was grieving or in distress. This time, she found herself somewhat at a loss for words and quietly sat back in her chair, leaving it up to Adam to comfort their neighbor. She was perplexed that this man who'd been so continually abused by his wife would be so overcome with grief by her death. After a while, she turned to Frank and asked, "Have you spoken with your daughter? Have you told her what has happened? Perhaps she could come here and stay with you until you feel better. It might help to have someone who knows you be close by."

Frank looked up at Eve and quietly responded. "No. I haven't said a word to her. She never cared much for Olive and I really don't want to upset her with bad news. She has enough to take care of. I really don't want her to come here. Anyway, I think, for now, I'd rather be by myself." Eve thought Frank appeared somewhat frightened when the subject of his daughter was brought up and thought it best not to say anything more.

"It's better to look ahead," said Adam, trying his best to be supportive. He glanced at Eve, waiting for her to add some words of condolence, but she remained quiet, just fingering her napkin.

"You're right," sobbed Frank, wiping his eyes with the corner of a handkerchief, "but it's very hard and will take some time." Then, he excused himself and said he thought he should leave. "Right now, I think it's best for me to be alone." His eyes were filled with tears as he rose from the table, then turned to politely thank Eve for the dinner.

"We'll do this again when you're feeling better," she responded as she rose and began to clear the table. As she went into the kitchen, Adam led his neighbor to the door and followed him out to the edge of the front patio.

"Thank you," murmured Frank, "Sorry I spoiled your evening."

Adam looked out at the dark desolate prairie that stretched beyond the little houses, then replied softly, "You didn't spoil anything. Don't worry about it. Just take care of yourself now. Go to bed now and get some rest. I'll stop by tomorrow to see how you're doing." Adam felt certain that, if given the chance, Frank would want to talk about his feelings at some point and he knew that his support would be needed.

When he reentered the house, Adam sought out his wife, who'd retreated to the bedroom and asked, "What's wrong, Eve? You hardly said a word all evening."

Turning to face her husband, Eve exchanged her thoughts for carefully chosen words. "I don't know exactly how to explain it, but I have a very strong feeling that something is wrong," she stated slowly, but firmly.

Adam waited for an explanation, but none came. What do you mean?" he finally asked.

"Well," she began slowly, "I was in the pool today. You wouldn't believe how many people were there...I've never seen it so crowded."

"Yes...And?"

"Well, the gossip was flying and I did my best to stay out of it, but I overheard one woman say that, about a month ago, she and Olive were in the pool together. She said Olive was complaining about a headache, so the woman offered her an aspirin, but Olive refused and went into a lengthy explanation as to why she didn't believe in pills. Even though she had a lot of pain, she didn't even take anything for her arthritis. She claimed the only medicine she ever took was a cough drop now and then if she had a sore throat and that was rare."

"I'm afraid to ask any further," replied Adam, disturbed by the direction their conversation had taken.

"Well, they found Valium in Olive's body, didn't they?" Eve asked rhetorically. "It doesn't make sense. If Olive wouldn't even take an aspirin, why on earth would she take Valium? Something is wrong."

"Maybe she didn't want anyone to know she was taking it. It's not uncommon for people to do a lot of things in private that they'd rather keep secret and not talk about to others. I don't think Olive would have wanted anyone to know about her habits, especially if they had to do with medications," Adam pointed out.

"You may be right, but did you ask Frank if Olive ever took Valium?" she persisted.

"No...I didn't. I didn't think it was any of my business."

"Well, it does raise a question."

"Let it be," interrupted Adam. "I don't want to upset Frank any further. It was bad enough having to be the one to tell him that his wife was dead."

"Yes," said Eve, softening, "that certainly was very brave of you. I know it must have been difficult." She put her arm around her husband's shoulder.

"I've had more experience with that sort of thing than most people. I can't tell you how many times I've had to break sad news to family members...it's very hard."

"I understand...it's never easy, is it?"

"Especially this time. I feel very sorry for Frank. He's trying his best to hide his feelings, but I can tell he's very upset. I think I'll go over there tomorrow. I'm worried about him. I don't like the fact that he's all alone."

"You're very kind, Adam." Eve looked admiringly at her husband.

As they were preparing to go to bed, Eve turned to Adam and remarked, "it's been so quiet here lately...kind of strange not to hear Olive screaming, but it's something I think I can get used to."

"Don't tell me you miss it," replied Adam.

"No, of course not. It's just that the silence makes me realize how much a part of our lives she had become. You know, sometimes what you don't hear can be as disturbing as what you do hear." Then, changing the subject, she added, "when you go to see Frank tomorrow, you might want to ask him about the Valium."

Adam looked at Eve, but didn't say a word. He simply grunted, then fluffed his pillow and slid into bed. *Well,* thought Eve, as she rolled over, *there are still a few things that need to be clarified and if he isn't going to ask any questions, then I suppose it's up to me.*

Chapter 5

The following morning, Eve awakened later than usual, having spent a restless night rehashing the discovery of Olive's body and all the conversations that she heard at the pool. *How ironic*, she thought. *Even in death, Olive managed to disturb the tranquility she felt she desperately needed.* The sun was streaming through the sliding glass door and, to her surprise, she found herself on Adam's side of the bed. Neither he nor Coco were in the room. Eve couldn't exactly pinpoint what was bothering her, but she sensed the familiar nagging sensation in the back of her mind that signaled things were not what they appeared to be. Over the years, she'd learned that it was best to trust these feelings. Not wanting to waste any more time, she threw back the covers and pushed herself out of bed.

After brushing her teeth and washing her face, Eve threw on a pair of slacks and a loose fitting blouse. As she made her way into the kitchen, she noticed Adam and Coco, who were sitting in the den, Adam at his desk with Coco on top of his feet. "You're off to a late start," Adam remarked, as he looked at his watch.

"I thought I'd sleep in this morning and wait until it warmed up a bit before going for a swim." Even though she wasn't completely honest, Eve felt the explanation seemed quite logical. Almost as an afterthought, she asked, "Didn't you say you were going to see Frank today?"

"Yes. As a matter of fact, I was just about to go over there now." Eve grabbed her bag and followed Adam as he headed for the front door. He led the way down the sidewalk and waited for her at the mailbox, "Enjoy the swim," he said, grinning broadly.

"Thank you...I will," replied Eve, ignoring the slight tone of sarcasm she detected in her husband's voice. She walked at a brisk pace, wondering what she might find out. She didn't even know what she was looking for, but, whatever it was, she was sure the pool was the most logical place to begin an inquiry. As she anticipated, a row of golf carts was neatly lined up along the street in front of the entrance to the pool. Even before she reached the gate, she heard loud voices and laughter coming from inside. At least things seem to be getting back to normal, perhaps even a bit more than normal, she reflected, as she entered and saw a cluster of people gathered around the pool. The crowd was even larger than the one she'd seen the previous morning. *Were these people merely curious*, she wondered, *or did they too sense that something wasn't quite right?*

For the first time since she began coming to the pool, Eve had difficulty finding a chair. She made her way through the throng, said "good morning" at least a half dozen times, then stopped to stare in amazement at all the activity that surrounded her. Conversations were in full swing and voices reverberated like the buzzing of insects.

"We're damn lucky to be living in America," said one woman. "I saw on television how the Japanese are shipping their retirees off to Australia. Can you imagine...you live all your life in one place, then they ship you off to a totally foreign country where people don't even speak the same language. Damn lucky to be living here, that's what I think."

Eve could always spot the men and women who were unhappy, those who were not in harmony with their environment. Male or female, they were the ones who moved about clumsily, scraping their chairs as they dragged them across the concrete. They were also the ones whose voices could be heard above the others, talking louder than necessary. She could sense when a quarrel over space was about to break out, for these folks were always ready to argue. *Fortunately,* she thought, *the restless ones usually moved on and didn't stay very long in Sunshine Valley...that is, except for Olive.*

Weaving her way through the crowd as gracefully as possible, Eve looked around for signs of someone who was preparing to leave. Unfortunately, most people appeared to have settled in for the day. Even though it was against the rules, some had even brought picnic baskets filled with food and drinks. Now that the unofficial pool monitor was dead, it seemed that rules were being broken right and left. As she made her way around the pool, Eve passed a very large man who was obviously uncomfortable. He moved awkwardly and uneasily and looked as if he was ready to collapse any minute. *That's all we need,* she thought, *another dead body in the pool.*

Eventually, Eve spotted an empty chair in the farthest corner. She eased her way towards it, trying her best to avoid stepping on legs and oily backs. Placing her towel on the chair, she sat down and began to survey the chaotic scene. As she looked around, Eve felt as if she'd entered an alien world. The row of plastic lounge chairs that encircled the pool was filled with bodies in various stages of undress. Some of the bathers were wrapped in an assortment of brightly colored terrycloth robes. Others had bared themselves as much as propriety allowed and had begun, in great seriousness, to smear their bodies with a variety of ointments. She was surprised at the number of bodies that were covered with tattoos and wondered for a moment if she should suggest that Adam get one. *No, she thought, whatever the design, she wouldn't want to look at it every day.* The smell of coconut floated through the air. Amid the splashes of pinks and blues and yellows, Eve noticed Pearl Thomas who made a more lackluster appearance in her dark green flannel gown and somber expression. She seemed ill at ease in the midst of all the lively activity.

It must be spring break, thought Eve, as she noticed a small group of teenage boys and girls sitting around the pool. One boy in particular caught her attention. His broad shoulders and muscular build revealed the body of a first-class athlete. He looked at Eve and smiled, then walked over to the deep end of the pool and made a perfect dive, hardly creating a splash. When he hoisted himself out of the water near Eve's chair, she couldn't restrain herself. "Very impressive," she said, grinning.

All of a sudden, Eve's observations were interrupted by a woman who was waving a towel and calling her name. It was Peggy Walsh, a pool regular and long-time resident of Sunshine Valley. She returned the woman's greeting. Without the slightest difficulty, she began tiptoeing her way through the boisterous crowd and walked over to Eve. "Well, I see you always know where to find the action," Peggy said, as she tried to avoid a straw basket. "I haven't seen this place so animated in all the time I've lived here. Where did all these people come from?"

"You're right...I've never seen it so packed," responded Eve.

"Maybe what this place needed was a good drowning. At least it seems to have sparked some life back into people."

"I must say, you certainly seem to be in good spirits today, Peggy."

"Yes...I'm feeling pretty good. And you? What brings you here? You don't usually like the crowds."

"I thought I'd get in some exercise, but now, I'm not so sure." Eve felt she sounded unconvincing and was certain Peggy picked up on her uneasiness.

"Why not? The pool's more or less empty today, isn't it? I don't think most people have come here to swim. They're only interested in the gossip and believe me," she said, lowering her voice, "there's plenty of it. You wouldn't believe everything I've heard."

At first, Eve pretended to be unconcerned, but then decided to abandon all pretense with this garrulous woman who seemed more than eager to talk. After all, she was looking for some answers, wasn't she? "Pull up a chair, Peggy...please...sit down and let's have a nice talk."

"You must be reading my mind," the woman replied, grabbing a nearby chair that had just been vacated.

Well, Eve thought, *this is going to be easier than I anticipated.* If there's one person who knows what's happening in Sunshine Valley, it's Peggy Walsh.

"I saw Alice Webber this morning," said Peggy. "Poor thing. She still hasn't gotten over the shock of finding Olive in the Jacuzzi. It really hit her hard."

"Oh, yes...I've been meaning to go over to her house and see how she's doing," replied Eve. "I know she was quite upset, but I haven't had a chance to talk to her yet."

"I'm afraid you're too late. She's leaving today to go back home...Wisconsin, I think. Such a nervous woman. She can't wait to get out of here. All of this has been too much for her and, I must say, I can't really blame her." Then, without skipping a beat, Peggy asked, "Have you seen Frank Howell lately?"

"Well, actually, yes. He came over for dinner last night."

"And?" Peggy looked at Eve with anticipation, waiting to hear more.

"Well, nothing really. I don't know him very well and he didn't have much to say. He was pretty quiet the whole evening. Adam feels sorry for him and told me he's been very depressed. Even though she wasn't particularly nice to him, from the little I gathered, it sounds as if Frank really misses Olive."

To this, Peggy made a clicking sound with her tongue and said, "I'll bet he does." She moved in closer and Eve could feel the woman's warm breath on the side of her neck. She paused a moment, then whispered, "Word has it...he killed her. That's what I heard. That's what a lot of folks around here are saying. They think he finally got fed up with all her complaining and did her in."

This time it was Eve who hesitated, "That's preposterous! What makes you think she was killed, anyway? Her death was ruled an accident. Besides, Frank was playing golf when Olive died. That's where Adam found him....at the golf course. He couldn't have killed his wife." Eve looked at the woman, expecting her to agree, but this was not to happen.

"I don't think most people blame him, however," the woman continued, ignoring Eve's defense. Then, as she surveyed the thirty-odd people who were sitting or standing around the pool, she took a deep breath and sighed, "Sometimes I feel like a tourist here, don't you?"

"Yes. I know what you mean. You don't really get to know people very well. They come and go and keep pretty much to themselves when they're here." Eve had often expressed these same feelings to Adam. She thought that people in Sunshine Valley were rather remote, as if parts of their minds were always somewhere else. But, as he would explain in his logical fashion, that's because nobody is *from* Sunshine Valley. They're all from somewhere else.

"Retirement," exclaimed Peggy sarcastically, "the wonderful life...so carefree. Hah!" She looked around and made a sweeping gesture. "It's just people, doing nothing, isn't it? Some of them are nicer than others...but, they're pretty much the same as anywhere else." Shaking her head, she turned back to Eve and confided, "my own personal feeling, of course, is that Raul killed Olive."

The high-pitched voices of the women standing around the pool rose in peaks above the flat male monotones. For a moment, Eve was speechless, not certain that she'd heard correctly. "Peggy, did you say what I think you said? You think Raul killed Olive? First of all, why do you believe someone actually killed Olive? And why Raul? The coroner's report ruled her death an accident, not murder. As far as I know, nothing has changed. Have you heard anything different?"

The woman shook her head again and began to explain her reasoning. "Do you think they care? One dead old lady? Besides, it would be bad for business. The police don't want to stir things up. How do you think that would look? Murderer on the loose in Sunshine Valley. Nobody would want to come here and live. Besides, we don't even have a real sheriff in this town. Bud Warner's only a deputy. He's had the job for less than a year and what are his qualifications? From what I hear, he used to sell insurance...that's what he did. He only got the job of deputy because he's a friend of the sheriff in Tucson. They're way too busy rounding up car smugglers and trying to stop people from illegally crossing over the border to worry about some harmless retired folks in Sunshine Valley. Besides Bud and a handful of senior-citizen volunteer assistants, what kind of official protection do you think we have here? I doubt if anyone of them is capable of dealing with a real killer."

She does have a point, thought Eve. The lack of professional law enforcement was singularly noticeable in Sunshine Valley. "But, if it's true that Olive's death wasn't accidental, and I'm still not so sure you're right about that...what makes you think Raul killed her?" Eve persisted. Even though she might not agree with the woman's speculation, she was intrigued and wanted to hear more.

"Well, for one thing, nobody has seen him for at least a week. As far as I can determine, the last time somebody did see him was on the morning that Olive died. Tom Wicks said he heard Olive yelling at Raul when he was delivering mail and passed by the pool. She was probably threatening to report him again. I mean, we all knew Raul was here illegally, but nobody seemed to care...nobody but Olive, that is. She was always after him. You know how emotional these Mexicans can get. I think he probably finally had enough, so he killed her, and then dumped her body in the Jacuzzi to make it look like an accident."

"Did Tom say he saw Raul?" Eve asked.

"I think so. Well...I'm not sure he actually saw him, but he heard enough to know it was Raul she was yelling at. She was constantly after him and he probably finally had enough of her insults and threats and just offed her. They'll never find him though."

"No? Why's that?"

"Probably somewhere back in Mexico by now. At least, that's where I'd be if I were in his shoes. I certainly wouldn't stick around here and wait to be arrested. He probably just ran away as fast as he could."

Eve had heard that Raul had a strong disliking for Olive, but she wasn't as certain as Peggy that this feeling extended to murder. "How well did you know Olive?" she asked.

"Well enough to know that she wasn't someone I wanted to get close to. You can't go prying into other people's lives the way she did and expect to be liked. Folks don't go for that...not here anyway. That woman was a real troublemaker and I'm willing to bet you won't find one person in all of Sunshine Valley who would defend her actions."

"Yes, I think you're probably right. I never heard anyone say a positive word about her." Eve seldom had difficulty talking, but Peggy's assertions about Raul left her speechless.

"One other thing," said Peggy, in a whisper that was barely audible. "Perhaps I shouldn't even tell you, but I think you ought to hear it from me rather than from someone you don't know as well." She sat up and looked around at all the bodies surrounding the pool, then continued. "I don't see him now, but there was a man here earlier who even suggested that you and Adam might have killed Olive..."

Stunned by Peggy's words, Eve bolted upright. "What? You can't be serious. We're the ones who found Olive..." She didn't know how to respond other than deny everything she heard.

"That's exactly why the man thought you might be guilty," Peggy continued. "He said he has a friend who's a policeman in Chicago and this friend told him that, quite often, a person who claims to have discovered a dead body is really the killer and just wants to throw people off the track by claiming he found the corpse."

Eve didn't let her finish. "That's absolutely crazy...Adam and I had nothing whatsoever to do with

Olive's death. In fact, we both tried to stay out of her way as much as possible."

"Don't get me wrong...I don't think you had anything to do with her death, but I just wanted to let you know what I heard before you hear it from somebody else. As for Olive, I tried to avoid her as much as possible myself," Peggy continued, looking directly at Eve. "Every now and then, I'd see her in the pool. Like clockwork. She'd come around nine, go in the dressing room, hang her robe on the same hook, then take a shower. If she was at the pool when I was there, I tried my best to avoid talking to her. But, that wasn't always possible. I came early once and caught her washing her hair in the shower. She looked like she was either going to kill me or drop dead right there on the spot. You're not supposed to use the shower to wash your hair, you know, but I caught her. How she must have hated me for that! Usually, though, when other people were around, she would just take a quick shower. Sometimes, she didn't even look wet when she came out. After she finished showering, she'd walk over to the guest book and sign in, then take off her slippers and line them up neatly under the table. She said she didn't want to get water on them. She never stayed in the pool very long and would paddle back and forth for a few minutes. Not much of a swimmer, mind you...after she finished, she'd go sit in the Jacuzzi. That she loved to do. She could sit there for half an hour sometimes...Most of the time, she had it to herself, because anyone who knew her didn't want to join her...she'd sit there, humming to herself and looking like she was scheming something new."

Eve was transfixed by Peggy's description of Olive's routine. Suddenly, she pulled her chair forward and demanded, "Tell me again. What did she do when she would come out of the dressing room?"

Not fully grasping the importance of her account, Peggy slowly repeated, "Like I said, she'd walk over to the guest book, sign in, then get in the pool, paddle back and forth..."

"No," Eve interrupted, "the slippers...you said she would take off her slippers and put them under the table by the guest book?"

"Yes, that's right. She always had the same routine, but..."

Again, Eve interrupted the woman. "Are you certain Olive always did the same thing with her slippers?" she asked anxiously.

"Yes, I'm quite sure. I remember one day somebody kicked them away and she became furious because she couldn't find them right away."

Eve looked at Peggy's face, but didn't say a word. She was stunned by what her friend had just told her. Without any explanation, she abruptly sprang to her feet and began folding her towel. "Well, Peggy, I better be getting home," she said as she turned to leave. "It's getting a little too crowded for me here."

"Did I say something wrong? I hope I didn't upset you. I didn't mean to imply that you and Adam had anything to do with..." Peggy seemed perplexed by her friend's sudden departure.

"No, Peggy, don't worry, I'm fine." Eve didn't let her finish. "It's just that it's later than I realized and I suddenly remembered that I'm supposed to go into town with Adam. I'll see you again soon, though...and thank you for all the news." *Thank you indeed*, she thought. Eve began reviewing everything her friend had just told her. She always felt she was too sensible to be influenced by gossip and innuendo. Lately, however, after all the stories she'd heard, she feared she was slowly losing her ability to distinguish reality from fiction. One fact she knew was indisputable. She and

Adam had nothing to do with Olive's death and she decided she'd spare telling her husband about the accusations that were being made against them. She knew he'd get furious and that wouldn't help anybody. No, the news about the slippers was much more important. Softly, she began repeating the German phrase that had taken on new meaning for her—"unter den pantofeln."

As he was walking towards Frank's house, Adam wondered what he was going to say to his friend. Having been a hospital administrator for over thirty years, he had often witnessed the suffering and sorrow of people who lost loved ones. More times than he would have wished, he'd sat with mothers, fathers, husbands, and wives, trying to provide words of comfort. Although he was accustomed to the role, he never really felt at ease in it. Because he sensed that Frank wanted to talk about his feelings, Adam knew he would open up if given the chance. *Perhaps this was what the man needed more than anything,* thought Adam, *someone he trusted that he could talk to.*

There was a long pause before Frank responded to the front door bell.

"I'm sorry," said Adam when his friend appeared, stooped over and unshaven. "Perhaps I've come at a bad time."

"There's never a good time," Frank responded, dryly. "Come in." He stepped back into the shadows and motioned for Adam to enter. The heavy drapes were drawn tightly, causing the house to seem darker than usual. Only a thin shaft of light penetrated the room through the amber-colored window panes that framed the front door. The smell of cat food filled the air.

"I've been thinking about you, Frank, and I'm concerned. I thought you might want to talk...sometimes it helps to let things out," said Adam in a low voice.

Frank's expression, usually mild and cheerful, was blank. After a few moments of silence, he looked up at Adam and solemnly declared, "I killed her." He appeared to have difficulty speaking, as if he hadn't used his voice in a while. From time to time, he made curious gurgling noises that sounded as if was trying to stifle a cough.

Adam put his arm around Frank and tried to lead him to a chair, but Frank shook his head and walked into the kitchen instead, leaving Adam standing bewildered, in the middle of the living room. When he returned, he was holding a bottle of pills. He screwed up his face in anguish and held out the plastic container in his trembling hand.

Frank began to sob uncontrollably. For the first time since Olive's death, he was able to openly express the sorrow that he'd been building up inside him. "It's me. I did it. I gave Olive the Valium," he confessed, as he shook the small vial. The corners of his mouth began to twitch.

This was an admission that Adam had not anticipated and it made him feel very uncomfortable. "You did? You gave her Valium?" he asked calmly, trying to hide his surprise.

"Yes, and I gave it to her every day, for months. I thought it would help calm her down. She never knew...never even suspected. It was me...I find this so difficult to say, but I'm afraid it was me...I'm the one who killed her." Frank's lips were quivering as he explained how he administered the drug to his wife. "She always drank a cup of coffee in the morning...I would crush a tablet into a powder and then mix it in...I did this every morning and she never knew...never suspected anything." A twisted grin spread across his face, followed by a new burst of tears that began streaming down his cheeks.

"Go ahead, Frank, just let it out. You'll feel much better if you let everything out. I'm here for you." Adam tried to sound encouraging, but realized there was very little he could do or say to comfort his friend and simply offered him a handkerchief.

"Did you hear me?" Frank demanded. Now, he was almost screaming. "I gave her the Valium. I'm the one who killed her." Again and again, he repeated the same words, then added, "but, it was an accident. You have to believe me...it was an accident. I didn't mean to kill her. I just wanted her to be calm. I thought the Valium would help her." His voice was straining and began to crack.

"Yes...I understand. I know you never meant to hurt her and I'm positive you never meant to kill her." Stunned by the startling revelation he'd just heard, it was all Adam could bring himself to say.

Frank took several quick, spasmodic steps as he backed away from Adam, then came forward again. "You must believe me, Adam," he begged, gasping for air. "It was an accident. I'm not making it up."

Again, Adam did his best to reassure his distraught friend. "Don't worry, Frank. I do believe you."

"You do? You really believe me?" Frank sounded surprised.

"Yes...I do. I really do believe you," replied Adam with greater conviction.

"How can I live with this? I'm so ashamed. Now, do you understand why I didn't want to say anything to my daughter about what happened? I don't want her to come here and find out that her father's a killer." Frank no longer looked sad, just frightened.

Adam wasn't sure how to answer his friend. None of the usual words of condolence seemed appropriate. After a few moments, he managed to collect his thoughts. "I know you made life easier for Olive," he said, choosing his words carefully. "She was a very troubled woman. At least you can hold on to the fact that you did your best to make her life a little easier. You never hit her and you never even raised your voice to her. You were very kind to her." He wished he could find something more meaningful to say, but, at that moment, he was at a loss. "Have you told anyone else about this?" he asked after a moment's silence.

"No...only you. I'm so ashamed...I couldn't tell anyone else...I don't think anyone would understand," Frank whimpered.

"Well, let's keep it that way. I think it's best. There's nothing more that can be done now. You must listen to me...do not tell anyone else what you just told me. I know it seems difficult, but believe me, you'll feel better about everything in time. I know you will."

Frank looked pale and shaken. "I really did it this time, didn't I?"

"Believe me, Frank, it wouldn't do Olive any good...or you, for that matter, to reveal this to anyone. Promise me you won't say a word about it to anyone else." When the man made no attempt to answer, Adam shook him slightly. "Promise me," he repeated.

Frank stopped sobbing for a moment, blew his nose, then smiled faintly at Adam. "All right, I promise" he replied faintly. "I won't say a word to anyone else."

"It's not as if you're trying to cover up a crime," Adam pointed out.

"Thank you," Frank replied, wiping his eyes. After a few moments, he looked up at Adam and said in a quivering voice, "There's something else. I want you to take a look at this." He led Adam over to a table and slowly opened a large suitcase. It was filled with cash. From where Adam was standing, he could only see stacks of what appeared to be hundred dollar bills.

"I just found this. I know Olive had money, but I never knew she kept so much cash in the house. I haven't counted it, but I think there must be several thousand dollars. I have no idea where it came from. The only place I could think of is the casino, but, as far as I know, she only went there once or twice."

Suddenly, Adam became aware of the oppressiveness of the house. He didn't think he could tolerate any more revelations. "Would you like to step outside for a bit? Maybe go for a walk? I think the fresh air would be good for you," he said to Frank, then began pacing around the room.

"No, thanks. I think I'll be okay now. You're right...it helps to talk. I'm starting to feel much better," Frank replied softly.

"Are you sure?"

"Yes. I need to go through some things. I'll be okay...really." Frank tried to force a smile, but began coughing instead.

"You could do those things later. There's plenty of time. It would be good for you to get out of the house," Adam persisted.

"No. I need to get ready for California. I have to get things in order...and the sooner the better." He stopped sobbing, but his face was still flushed, eyes bloodshot. "Thank you for listening to me, Adam...I really appreciate your friendship," he said, puffing out his cheeks. "I don't have anyone else."

Adam moved slowly towards the front door, followed closely by Frank. "It's okay," he said. "You know where to find me when you need me...any time, night or day...I'm always here for you." Once outside, the fresh air and bright sunshine stunned him for a moment. He walked slowly towards his house, filled with mixed feelings about what he'd just heard. For a brief moment, he even wondered if Frank really did intentionally kill his wife, then pushed aside the disturbing thought. Looking up, he saw Eve who was racing towards him.

"Adam...Adam," she called out breathlessly, "I have something important to tell you. Come inside..." Eve grabbed her husband's arm and led him up the sidewalk. "Quickly," she urged. "This is important."

"What's the rush? Are you okay? Has something happened?"

"Yes...yes...I'm fine. Come inside...quickly."

Eve led Adam into the house, then slammed the door and tossed her bag onto a chair. "I was at the pool," she began with a burst of excitement.

"Yes, I know," Adam said calmly.

"Well, I was at the pool when, all of a sudden it hit me. I realized that Olive's death was not an accident." Eve stood in the middle of the room, hands on hips, waiting for a response, but Adam had turned his back to avoid her gaze. After what Frank had just revealed, he feared what his wife might have to tell him. "Didn't you hear me?" she asked, receiving no reply to her disclosure.

"Yes...I heard you. I'm just not sure I understand you. What makes you think it wasn't an accident?" Adam asked cautiously.

"Well," she began, "something has been bothering me, something about the pool. I've had this gnawing feeling, but haven't been able to put it into words. Now I know what's been troubling me."

"Yes? And what's that?" Adam's curiosity began to increase.

"When we found Olive's body, one of her slippers was in the Jacuzzi, the other one was on the cement, next to the Jacuzzi."

"Yes, I know. So? What does that have to do with anything?" Adam asked.

"Well," replied Eve, "As you know, I went to the pool today and from what I learned, before Olive would go for a swim or a dip in the Jacuzzi, she would always leave her slippers under the table by the guest book."

"How do you know that?"

"Peggy Walsh told me. She said she'd seen Olive at the pool many times and that she was a woman who always followed the same routine. After signing in, she would leave her slippers by the guest book so they wouldn't get wet. She did this without fail. But, the morning we found her body, one of her slippers was on the concrete and the other one was in the Jacuzzi. She didn't follow her usual routine. I'm sure that means somebody was there with her, somebody who..." She broke off, suddenly realizing the meaning of her own words. "My God, Adam, somebody may have actually killed Olive," she gasped.

Adam was not prepared to discuss the possibility that Olive's death was actually murder and was less than overjoyed by his wife's conclusion.

"It doesn't mean Olive was killed by someone, just because her slippers were in a different place," he explained, trying to sound objective.

"Oh, Adam," sighed Eve, shaking her head in exasperation, "sometimes you're so infuriating." She turned and walked out of the room. Adam stood watching her. He was perplexed. Nothing that he'd heard in the past hour made any sense to him.

Chapter 6

Spring had arrived early in Sunshine Valley and the landscape was beginning to take on a new color. *What a beautiful morning,* Eve thought, as she looked out at the flowers that were starting to bloom. Such a shame that most of the 'snowbirds' were leaving just when the desert was about to show its real beauty. Patches of bright reds and yellows appeared almost overnight on the prickly bushes and shrubs that, a few days earlier, had seemed so lifeless.

"I'm going over to Frank's house now to feed the cat," she announced to Adam as she walked into the den.

Overwhelmed by everything he'd heard the previous day, when he awoke, Adam decided to put all thoughts of Frank and Olive out of his mind, at least for a while. He knew exactly how to accomplish this. The first thing he did after finishing his breakfast and going for a walk with Coco was to take out his stamp collection. He spread several large volumes across the desk, carefully turning one page after another. As Eve entered the room, he glanced up from the pile of books and seemed surprised to see her. "I thought you'd already gone," he said.

"I started to go, but got a little sidetracked." Eve stood quietly in the doorway, waiting to hear some cautionary words of advice, but quickly realized that Adam had nothing more to say. He was deeply involved in his research. She recognized the faraway sound of his voice and thought it best to leave him undisturbed.

Actually, she wasn't even sure what she wanted to hear from him. A simple word of reassurance would do, but there was just silence.

Eve was doing her best to postpone going over to Frank's house. After doing a few minor chores, she ran out of excuses and thought she better see that the cat had enough to eat. She wondered why she felt so uneasy and as she looked at Adam, deeply involved in his work, she shrugged her shoulders and decided she was being overly sensitive.

"See you in a while," Eve called out to her husband, not waiting for a response. She picked up the key Frank had given them, then left through the patio. Noticing the empty bird feeder, she paused for a moment, picked up a bag and scattered some seeds on the dish. She turned and went out the back gate, crossed the narrow path, and walked directly over to Frank's house. *How serene and peaceful everything appeared,* she thought...like a very secure, small oasis...certainly not a site for murder. In the sparkling air and brilliant sunshine of the Sonoran desert, her worries seemed out of place.

Eve tried to keep her mind focused on feeding the cat and avoided acknowledging the gnawing sense of apprehension she'd felt all morning. "Hello, Petticoat. It's only me," she called out in a voice louder than normal, as she entered the house. Hesitating for a moment in the middle of the living room, she looked around for some sign of life. All she heard was the low humming of the refrigerator in the kitchen. The house was dark and musty and, for an instant, she almost gagged at the mixture of cat odors and stale food that permeated the air. Quickly, she walked over to the drapes, pulled them open, then slid back the heavy glass door.

"Let's get some fresh air in here," she said, almost choking.

Eve thought Olive's absence in the house was quite apparent. A thick layer of dust had settled on the furniture and a stack of old newspapers was piled high on the couch. Wedged between two cushions, almost unnoticeable, a gray cat had curled itself into a fluffy ball.

"There you are, Petticoat. I'll bet you'd like something to eat." The half-sleeping animal opened and closed its eyes and began to purr as Eve leaned over to pet it. "Come on, little girl. Let's see if we can find something you like." The cat stretched her legs, yawned, then raised herself slowly and followed Eve into the kitchen. Frank had left an assortment of cat food on the table, along with written instructions on what to feed the animal.

"Well," said Eve, grimacing at the dried up food on the floor, "this doesn't look very appetizing." She picked up the bowl and flushed the contents down the disposal. "Let's try tuna this time." She opened a fresh can and scooped out half of the meat into a clean bowl. Petticoat sniffed, looked up at Eve, sniffed again, then decided sleep was more to her liking at the moment. "Oh, well, you'll be hungry later," she sighed. "I wonder if all of this turmoil hasn't affected you too."

Eve was struck by how clean the kitchen appeared, compared to the rest of the house. She hadn't known what to expect, but it seemed to her that Frank was at least making an attempt, however feeble, to reorganize his life. She wondered how Adam would manage if she weren't around. It wasn't a thought she liked to consider, but she couldn't help but make the comparison as she walked through the lonely house. For that matter, she wondered, how would she manage without Adam? Not very well, she concluded, realizing how much she'd grown to depend on him for so many things.

"Stop this," Eve whispered to herself. Once again, she tried to free her mind of unpleasant thoughts and forced herself to focus on the task at hand. *Perhaps she should leave some dry food in a dish,* she thought. Frank must have a box somewhere. She opened and closed one cabinet after another. Nothing but dishes and empty bottles. Turning around, she spotted a tall green chest that stood in the corner of the room. She hesitated, then walked over to it, and pulled open the door. For a moment, she felt like a snoop and this was a feeling she did not particularly enjoy. "Here it is," she said, pulling out the package of dried food. She poured a little into a bowl and placed it next to the tuna that she'd dished out.

When Eve went to replace the box, she couldn't help noticing the odd assortment of items that filled the cabinet—several boxes of candy, a half empty bottle of Canadian Club, even a handful of cigars. She smiled, realizing that she had discovered Frank's personal arsenal of treats. As she picked up a pair of women's reading glasses, she was reminded of what Adam had told her about Frank's tricks. She shuddered and, for a moment, had an odd sensation that Olive was standing behind her, watching her every move and laughing as she uncovered all of Frank's secrets.

Eve began moving objects and reading labels. *He sure has a sweet tooth,* she thought, as she picked up a bag of chocolates and shook it. She replaced it on top of the pile of boxes that were neatly stacked on the upper shelf and was about to close the cabinet door when she noticed a small bottle that was pushed back into a corner. Without thinking, she picked up the plastic container and shook it. *Some kind of tablets,* she thought, and was about to replace her find when she suddenly recalled the image of Olive floating in the Jacuzzi and what the coroner's autopsy had revealed. Her hands started to tremble as she opened the vial and poured out a few of the tablets. *Oh, my God*, she thought, *is this what I think it is? Can this possibly be?*. "Valium!" she exclaimed audibly and whirled around to see if anyone else was in the room. The picture of Olive's lifeless body swirling around in the hot steaming water grew stronger in her mind. She quickly replaced the pills and looked to make sure everything was just as she'd found it, before closing the cabinet door. Her heart started to pound as she raced to leave the house. She stopped for a moment, took a deep breath, then headed for the safety of the sunshine and fresh air.

"Adam...Adam!" shouted Eve, as she burst into the house and ran into the den. "You're not going to believe this..."

Adam was stunned by the abruptness of his wife's entrance. He pushed himself up from behind the desk and walked over to her. "What happened? What's wrong this time? Is Petticoat all right? Are you okay?"

Eve stood in the middle of the room, speechless. "Oh, Adam," she began to tremble. "Frank..."

"What about Frank?" interrupted Adam. From the sound of her voice, he feared something serious had happened to their neighbor.

"I was looking for some dry food to give the cat," Eve began. "Frank keeps her food in a separate cabinet...the same one where he hides...I mean hid things from Olive. Do you know which one I mean?"

"Yes...I do," Adam answered haltingly.

Eve eyed her husband suspiciously. She knew all too well when he was trying to conceal something. "Do you also know about the Valium that he keeps there?" Her stare was deep and penetrating.

Adam took a few steps back. "So that's where he kept it," he said in a subdued voice.

"You know about this?" Eve didn't wait for a response. "You know that Frank has a supply of Valium?" They both stood silently, looking at each other with anticipation. "I'm almost afraid to ask my next question," continued Eve.

"Sit down," said Adam, helping his wife into a chair. He pulled up another chair and sat next to her.

"I don't understand how you..." Eve was at a loss for words.

"Wait a minute," interrupted Adam. "Let me explain. Frank just told me about the Valium."

"And you didn't want to tell me?" Eve's mouth dropped.

"I wasn't purposely trying to hide anything from you. The reason I neglected to mention the Valium was that I didn't want to upset you and I didn't think it would help anyone."

"What do you mean...wouldn't help anyone? A woman has been murdered...the coroner found Valium in her and, apparently, she didn't take it herself...now, you tell me Frank gave it to her...what does that sound like to you?"

Again, Adam interrupted. "It wasn't murder. It was an accident...that's right...an accident. Frank told me he put tranquilizers in Olive's coffee, thinking it would calm her down...he did it for her own good. He didn't mean to harm her...and he certainly didn't mean to kill her. I'm sure of that." Eve stared at her husband as he continued to explain how Frank would regularly crush a tablet and mix it into his wife's morning coffee.

"And he thought that the Valium would make her more manageable?" she questioned, not fully grasping what Adam was telling her.

"Yes, he thought she'd be calmer and easier to deal with," Adam replied softly. "He's very upset now, fearing he may have been responsible for Olive's death. But, he's suffered enough for what happened...I think the best thing we can do is to forget about this. Let's just put it out of our minds." He looked at his wife, hoping she'd agree with his suggestion.

But Eve was in no mood to ignore what she'd just learned. "Where did he get the Valium?" she persisted.

"What?" he asked.

She repeated the question, but Adam was unable to provide an answer. It had never occurred to him, during his entire conversation with Frank, to ask him where he had obtained the pills.

"I have no idea. I was a bit stunned when he told me what he had done...I never thought to ask him," Adam replied, sheepishly.

After a few moments, Eve looked into her husband's eyes and stated firmly, "Listen to me carefully...Olive's death was *not* an accident."

"How can you be so sure?" Adam looked at his wife a little skeptically.

"The slippers," she replied without hesitation.

"What? The slippers don't mean anything. I don't know where you're headed with this line of thinking, but if somebody did kill Olive, I'm positive it wasn't Frank. Don't forget, he was at the golf course when she drowned." Even though Eve had not accused Frank directly, Adam felt a need to defend his friend.

Eve was quiet for the remainder of the afternoon. Once the shock of her discovery began to subside, she was able to understand Adam's reasons for keeping silent about the Valium. She did, however, have difficulty accepting the fact that he hadn't confided in her. But, in the end, she agreed with his decision. Even though she didn't approve of Frank's actions, she thought that it would be of no possible benefit to anyone to reveal them at this point. Following her husband's lead, she would keep the secret. *If Frank did kill his wife on purpose,* she thought, *he'd have to mete out his own self punishment. He would have to live the rest of his life with his guilt.*

In spite of all she'd learned, or perhaps because of it, Eve grew increasingly restless as the day wore on. What was it that troubled her so much, she wondered? What was it that wouldn't go away? Finally, at dinner, she broke her silence. "There's still something I can't seem to get out of my mind."

"I thought so. You've hardly eaten anything and you're usually not this quiet unless something is bothering you. Now, tell me, my little sleuth, what is it that you find so distressing?"

"You may find it amusing, but I know something isn't right and I can't seem to figure out what it is."

"Don't get so upset, darling. Perhaps I can help. What is it that's puzzling you? Does it have to do with Frank and the Valium?" Adam asked carefully.

"No, it has nothing to do with him. There's something about the pool area that still bothers me."

"You mean the slippers?"

"No. I know Olive didn't bring them over to the Jacuzzi and she certainly wasn't wearing them if she went into the water by herself. I'm pretty sure somebody else was there with her."

"Who might that be?" Adam asked gently.

"I don't know yet, but, there's something else." Eve didn't want to discuss the slippers again. She knew she was right and didn't want to get into an argument.

"Another clue?" As soon as he asked, Adam regretted his question.

"I know you think I'm silly, but there has to be an explanation for all of this and I'm quite certain it has to do with the pool area." Eve was adamant in her assertion.

"You seem to be getting more and more involved with Olive's death. I didn't think you particularly cared for her when she was alive, so I find it odd that you're focusing so much attention on her now that she's dead."

"You're right. Olive's blatant egotism and total disregard for other people repelled me. But, I don't believe her personality flaws or disgusting behavior justify murder, if, indeed somebody did kill her."

One thing was certain, thought Adam, *once Eve put her mind to something, there was no stopping her*. She never left a project unfinished and if she was searching for an answer, he was certain she would persist until she found it.

"It's probably right under my nose. That's what's so annoying," continued Eve. *Why can't I ever see things clearly when I'm supposed to?* she demanded of herself. A crime most certainly has been committed. Olive Howell was murdered, right here in Sunshine Valley, of that she was sure. Even though she wasn't particularly well liked, who hated Olive enough to actually want to kill her and why? These were the questions Eve felt needed to be answered.

Chapter 7

Eve spent another sleepless night, unable to put aside images of Olive, the slippers, the Jacuzzi, the tranquilizers she'd found in Frank's cabinet, and the confession he'd made to Adam. The plot was beginning to thicken. She tried to reconstruct the events leading up to the discovery of Olive's body. Over and over again, she retraced the steps that she and Adam had taken, starting from the moment they left the house to entering the pool area, but nothing seemed any clearer than it had the day before.

Within the past few days, Eve had become obsessed with someone she hardly knew and didn't even like, and now, this person had possibly...no, probably...been murdered. She wondered if anyone else in Sunshine Valley shared her doubts about the circumstances surrounding Olive's death. If they did, it didn't seem to matter. Despite a good deal of gossip, most people were going about their lives as if Olive never existed. Others were glad she was gone, regardless of the circumstances. Even Adam didn't seem to show much interest in his wife's suspicions. *Perhaps I should do the same as everybody else and forget about all this unpleasantness,* she said to herself. But, no, that wasn't possible.

When she awakened, it took Eve a few seconds to realize that Adam had already left the house. She remembered that, before he went to bed, he'd told her he would be leaving early for the library in Tucson to do some research on his stamp project. She looked at the clock and sighed. She must have fallen asleep some time towards morning. She wondered if Adam had been able to sleep through all her tossing and turning. If he hadn't, he didn't let her know. Reluctantly, she got up and dressed, pausing from time to time to look out the window. In the distance, the sky was darker than usual. *We might have rain today*, she thought, and hoped Adam wouldn't get caught in it.

Eve passed the morning on the patio, feeding the birds and planting orange African daisies along the edge of the wall. She felt unusually agitated and hoped the physical exercise would get her mind off this obsession with Olive, but, every so often, she found herself returning to the same set of events, trying to visualize how the unfortunate woman had spent her last morning alive. With Coco at her side, Eve stood back, wiped her forehead, and watched the roadrunners pick at the crumbs she'd placed on top of the stucco patio wall. The poodle's head jerked up and down, following the birds as they darted back and forth, eagerly snapping up the food. Forcing herself to sit down at the patio table, she took a sip of the coffee that had gone cold. She grimaced. Despite Eve's attempts to follow something resembling a normal routine, she found little enjoyment in anything she touched or looked at. With so many distracting thoughts on her mind, she didn't even feel like painting today.

At ten o'clock, Eve walked over to Frank's house. To her relief, the trip was uneventful. Petticoat had eaten everything she put out on her last trip, so she emptied the remaining can of tuna into the dish and poured out another helping of dried food. She lingered in the house a little longer than necessary and found herself thinking about Frank. So far, he was the only person she could identify as a possible murder suspect. Perhaps he killed his wife, but, by accident, as he maintained. If it weren't for the slippers, Eve felt she could let everything go. Admittedly, Frank said he was at the golf course when Olive drowned and that's where Adam found him when he went looking for him. *But,* she thought, *it could have been possible for him to come back, sneak into the pool without anyone seeing him, kill Olive, then drive back to the golf course.* Logically, it was possible, but intuitively, Eve felt it didn't make sense. It would have been too easy for someone to see him. Besides, why go to all that trouble when, if he'd wanted to do away with his wife, he could have easily carried out his intentions in the privacy of their own home?

True, Eve reasoned, Frank did have a motive for killing his wife. Olive had verbally abused him on a daily basis for years—under the slipper—and without her around, he stood to inherit a great deal of money that he could spend as he pleased. But, could he intentionally commit murder? Eve tried to visualize Frank sneaking up on Olive in the Jacuzzi and holding her head under the water. No, she decided, it didn't fit. It would have required too drastic a personality change for him to commit such a horrid act.

Well, at least now, one thing seemed clearer to Eve. Olive had definitely been murdered, but she felt quite certain that Frank was not the killer. As much as she disliked the so-called tricks he played on his wife, she was positive that Frank wasn't capable of intentionally murdering his wife. Like Mr. Dennis at her school, Frank was, if anything, only capable of committing petty crimes. *Men who do sneaky things*, she reflected, *are basically cowards*. They're too afraid of getting caught to ever do anything that requires bold action. No, a real killer was out there somewhere in Sunshine Valley, a person who was capable of bold action and, so far, this person was unknown. She shuddered at her own disturbing thoughts.

Within fifteen minutes, Eve was back in her own house and decided it was time for her to try and fill in some of the missing pieces of the puzzle that was haunting her every waking moment. She remembered seeing Paula and Doty's names in the guest book. Apparently, they were the first ones, at least officially, to arrive at the pool that morning. *If they were there when Olive arrived, perhaps they knew something and could shed some light on things,* she thought.

Eve looked through her recipe box, took out an index card and left the house again. She decided it might be worthwhile to pay a visit to the Irish sisters and do some investigating. As usual, the street was quiet as Eve made her way towards their house. Overhead, the sky was still clear and sunny, but, in the distance, gray clouds were steadily approaching. A golf cart came whirring down the street and passed her. The driver waved mechanically and she returned the greeting. Here and there, someone was working in a garden or washing a car. How neat and orderly everything seemed, but, Eve shuddered, realizing that behind this ordinary looking façade, an evil presence was lurking.

She hesitated for a moment as she put her finger on the door bell. Should she have called first? No. Wasn't part of her plan to appear spontaneous? After all, she wanted to discover as much as possible without seeming to pry.

"I suppose I should have called first," Eve announced, giving voice to her own misgivings, as Doty opened the door.

"Please...come on in. We're not doing anything special." The woman greeted her, as warm and friendly as ever.

"Paula," she shouted to her companion, "we have company."

The older woman emerged from the kitchen, wiping her hands on an apron.

"Hello, Eve. Come in. Just doing a little spring cleaning."

Eve couldn't tell if the woman was surprised to see her or if she simply had not heard the doorbell.

"Can I get you something?" Doty offered, as she ushered Eve into the house.

"No thanks. I was doing some cleaning myself and I came across the recipe for that chocolate cake you wanted, so, I thought I better bring it over before it slips my mind again."

Doty appeared confused, not fully grasping the reason for Eve's visit. After a few awkward moments of silence, a light of comprehension dawned in her eyes.

"Oh, yes, of course," the woman replied. "I forgot all about it as well."

"I know I promised you a while ago." With great difficulty, Eve forced herself to sound relaxed.

"Yes...that was such a good cake and Paula really loves chocolate."

The woman motioned to one of the two overstuffed chairs that stood against the wall. "Please...sit down," she offered.

Clutching the white index card in her right hand, Eve did as she was told. The room was warm and somewhat stuffy. She thought it odd that all the windows were closed in spite of the cool breeze outside. Because Paula and Doty had limited financial resources, their house was sparsely furnished. Looking around, Eve noticed a vase filled with a dozen long-stemmed roses. They were the focal point of an otherwise bare dining room table and seemed a curious contrast to the dreariness of the rest of the room.

"I've been meaning to bring you this recipe so many times," said Eve, "but, it seems that, as soon as I think of something these days, I forget it just as quickly. I'm afraid my mind isn't as sharp as it used to be."

"I know what you mean," responded Doty. "I'm becoming more forgetful myself. I left my bathing cap at the pool this morning and had to go back and look for it. Of course, it was still there. Nobody would want it anyway. I don't think there are too many bathing cap thieves in Sunshine Valley, do you?" She began to giggle.

"No, I think you're right about that," said Eve, hesitantly.

Despite her sixty-odd years, Doty's blue eyes still had an expression of youthful innocence about them. "Eve brought us the recipe for that chocolate cake you like," she announced to Paula who was slowly making her way across the room.

"I just love chocolate cake," the older woman acknowledged.

Her remark was followed by another moment of awkward silence. Realizing that she was still holding the recipe, Eve held out her hand to Doty who eagerly accepted the card.

"Are you sure I can't get you something? Coffee? Tea? Surely, there must be something I can offer." Doty seemed eager to please.

"No, thank you." *This is going nowhere,* thought Eve, as she pushed herself out of the chair. It's time for more direct action.

"By the way," she began, "I know this may seem a little strange, but I have been curious about something and was wondering if I could ask you a question?"

"Yes? What's that?" Doty asked innocently, while Paula moved closer in order to hear better.

"Well," began Eve, choosing her words carefully, "I've had a chance to look at the guest book by the pool and I noticed, on the morning that Olive drowned, you and Paula were the first ones to sign in."

Both of the women looked at each other simultaneously before responding, but it was Paula who took the lead.

"We were there early...very early...before Olive or anyone else got there...and, yes, I noticed that we were the first ones to sign in. I'm not sure if that means anything." Paula answered in a steady, confident tone, but nervously began tugging at a strand of gray hair on her forehead.

"Well, my reason for mentioning it is that I was wondering if you happened to notice anything *out of the ordinary that morning...that's all. Since you were there so early, did you happen to see anything that appeared unusual?"*

"Out of the ordinary? Unusual? Like what?" Doty asked innocently.

"No, we didn't see anything strange." Paul asserted. "Everything looked the same as always."

Eve watched the two women closely, searching for some indication of what they were really thinking. *Paula answered the questions quickly*, she thought, *perhaps too quickly.*

"Is something wrong?" asked Doty, apparently bewildered by her neighbor's question.

"Oh, no...of course not," Eve calmly reassured her, not wanting to appear anxious. "I guess it's just my natural curiosity...that's all. Since Adam and I were the ones who found Olive, I thought if there was anything unusual or different about that morning...if Olive seemed upset, disturbed about something..."

"Olive was always upset or disturbed about something," interrupted Paula.

"Yes, I know, but..." Eve didn't have a chance to finish her thought.

Suddenly, Doty seemed to come alive. "I know what people are saying. They think Frank killed her. Well, let me tell you one thing. It just isn't true. Frank would never commit such a horrible act. He would never kill his wife. He couldn't kill anyone. He's a very kind man." Doty's face turned bright red. She began to stutter, searching frantically for any words she could think of to defend Frank.

"Of course, Doty. I know that Frank is a kind man and I didn't mean to imply that he had anything to do with Olive's death." Eve calmly repeated words of reassurance, surprised at the response she'd elicited in the woman. Then, after an appropriate pause, she continued. "To make things clearer in my own mind, since you were the first ones at the pool, why don't you just tell me what you saw that particular morning."

Doty looked confused and turned to Paula, uncertain as to how she should respond.

The older woman calmly explained, "We were finished with everything and were about to leave when Olive arrived. She was alone and went into the dressing room. We didn't talk to her. We just left. That's all there is to it." Paula was firm and Doty nodded in agreement.

With some hesitancy, Eve continued questioning the women. "Did you happen to see anyone else outside the pool?"

"No, I don't think so." Doty appeared happy to reply.

"Are you sure you saw no one?" Eve pressed her.

"Wait...I'm trying to remember. Yes...Remember, Paula? Remember...we saw the mailman...yes, that's right...and that real estate agent...he was waiting in the car. I remember it now." Doty seemed pleased with herself for being able to recall so many details. Paula, however, remained quiet and began to play with her hair again.

Eve felt that she'd asked enough questions for the time being. She didn't want to arouse the women's suspicions or fears any further.

"You know," added Doty, "come to think of it, we saw Pearl Thomas too, but she didn't see us...at least, I don't think she saw us."

"Thank you. It was kind of you to answer my questions," Eve replied.

"Is something wrong?" Paula sounded worried.

"Oh, no. I'm simply curious. I like to see the whole picture. And now...I've taken up enough of your time." Eve started for the door. Then, turning to Doty, she said, "One last question...you didn't happen to see Raul, did you? He's such a good gardener and I haven't seen him around lately. We have a cactus in front of the house that I'd like him to do something about."

"No, we didn't," answered Paula without hesitation.

"Oh, yes, Paula," Doty exclaimed. "We did see him. He was working around the edge of the pool wall...remember? He came in a few minutes before Olive. I think he went into that little shed where he keeps his tools. We didn't notice him when we left though."

"Have you seen him lately? I really am anxious to locate him." Eve tried to conceal her desire to learn more.

"He hasn't been around here for days," Doty assured Eve.

"Well, no matter." Eve wondered if Doty was aware of the disapproving look her companion was giving her.

As she turned to open the door, Eve wished she could hear what these two women would have to say to each other after she was gone. Almost as an afterthought, she turned once again, but this time, she faced Paula. "Enjoy the cake. Let me know how you like it," she said in a loud voice.

Paula remained silent. Was she upset or had she not heard the comment? Doty followed Eve out of the house. Once she was far enough away from Paula, she whispered, "What Frank does with his own life is his own business. He's a good man and he didn't kill Olive."

"Yes, I'm certain you're quite right," Eve reassured her.

On impulse, she asked Doty if the roses were from Frank. Obviously taken by surprise, the woman stepped backwards and started to blush.

"Well, yes...actually, he did bring them over." She was stammering and seemed totally at a loss to provide a suitable explanation. She looked over her shoulder, hoping to find Paula, but there was no one to come to her rescue.

"They're beautiful," Eve said softly and patted her on the hand. Then, she turned and headed back home.

When she reentered the house, Doty was confronted by an agitated companion. "What do you think that was all about?" demanded Paula. She sounded almost petulant, but Doty knew she was more anxious than anything.

"She's simply curious," Doty said, repeating Eve's words, but she knew it would take some doing to really convince Paula.

"I hope she doesn't stir things up," said Paula briskly.

"No...that wouldn't do...would it?" Doty agreed,

Paula began pacing, then scolded, "You said way too much."

Doty was taken aback by this remark. She didn't like quarreling with her companion, mostly because she always lost any argument they had. "I didn't...but, I had to say something." She could barely get the words out.

"You didn't say anything about the Valium, did you?" Paula demanded.

"Of course not...I would never say anything about "

"What?" interrupted Paula as she strained to hear her companion's words.

"No," shouted Doty. "I didn't mention the Valium."

Paula walked over to Doty and grabbed the woman's wrists. The look on her face was stern. Doty had rarely seen her this upset. "Listen to me, Doty," she began, "you must never tell anyone about the Valium...not even Frank. I don't want him to know that we've noticed anything. You must promise me."

"But, are you sure he took the pills?"

"Of course, I'm sure. Who else could have taken them? Except for Eve, he's the only person who comes to the house and our supply seems to decrease after every one of his visits. If I'm not taking them and you say you're not taking more than usual, who else could it be?"

"Do you think...maybe he...?" Doty was on the verge of tears and couldn't finish her thought.

"It doesn't matter what either you or I think. Frank has always been very good to us. And don't forget, Olive was not a nice person. She got what she deserved. It was only a matter of time before she came to a bad end."

"I suppose you're right," Doty agreed, meekly. *Yes, she thought. Paula was always right about such things.*

"Now, I want you to forget about this. It's none of our business. We'll never speak of the matter again...understood?"

"Yes, Paula. I won't say another word. I just hope Frank doesn't get into trouble."

Doty began sobbing as Paula embraced her companion. "I'm sorry this upset you so much," she said, trying to comfort the younger woman. "Please, try not to worry. Everything will be okay, you'll see. But, for the time being, I think we should not have too much to do with Eve. It's better that way. She asks too many questions that I don't feel like answering."

As Eve walked down Camino Avion, she began mulling over everything she'd just heard. But, instead of going directly back home, she decided to go to the pool. She was bothered by the Irish sisters' account of what had happened on the morning of Olive's death. Why was Paula so reluctant to say anything? Were they covering up something? Did they have information about a possible murder? Were they protecting Frank in some strange way? Worse yet, did they have something to do with Olive's death? One unanswerable question after another raced through her mind. She wasn't prepared to accuse the women of outright lying, but she was quite certain they were hiding part of the truth, especially Paula. The older woman seemed to be on her guard, trying her best to give what she thought were the appropriate noncommittal answers to Eve's questions.

As far as most people in Sunshine Valley were concerned, Olive's death was an accident, at least according to the official report. People might have their doubts, but no one was certain that a murder had been committed. No one, that is, except for Eve and the actual killer. In an attempt to uncover some evidence, she made a concerted effort to reconstruct everything that had happened that morning. Who was the last person to see Olive alive? Was it Raul? Where was the gardener, anyway? Did Dave Wilcox see anything? Or the mailman? A lot of people had been in the area. Surely, somebody must have seen something that could shed light on the matter. If Olive hadn't been such a creature of habit, putting her slippers in the same place every time she went to the pool, even Eve might have conceded that her death was accidental.

Suddenly, Eve found herself standing in front of the gate that opened to the pool. She stopped, and for a moment, wondered what she should do next. Sounds of laughter and splashing water filled the air. She thought it distressing that people seemed to be having such a good time, pretending that everything was normal, when she knew very well that things were far from normal. She loathed the fact that even she had begun to act in ways that were inconsistent with her beliefs. It wasn't in her nature to pry into people's lives and to be telling so many lies. Let the dead rest in peace! Let Frank try to put his life together again! After all, didn't everyone agree that Olive got what she deserved? Mostly, it was the gossip, the suspicions, the half-whispered innuendos, that disturbed Eve. Olive and Frank had become public property. And now, even she was starting to turn over stones and poke about in private corners. It wasn't right, she chastised herself.

The gate was unlocked and Eve pushed it open. She looked around, then nodded to a man and woman who were about to enter the pool. How cheerful they appeared! She didn't know the people and, in a way, that was comforting, since she was in no mood to exchange superficial chatter. For a brief moment, she thought about sitting down, then, abruptly, she changed her mind. No, she decided, she'd had enough of this distasteful business for one morning and didn't want to hear any more gossip. She had to get away from the scene of the crime and so she did, quickly turning and dashing out the gate that she had just entered.

As Eve was walking down the street, she saw the realtor, Dave Wilcox, who was driving his car slowly towards her. He pulled into a driveway and stopped.

"Morning," he greeted cheerfully.

"Morning," Eve replied casually, somewhat annoyed that his car was blocking the sidewalk, forcing her to stop.

Dave Wilcox was a man in his late fifties. He was wearing white shoes, a light green polyester suit and a white belt that he hitched up as he walked around the side of the car.

"You wouldn't happen to know where I could find Frank Howell, would you?" he asked Eve. "I've tried calling him at all hours...but, no answer. Been to the house twice and nobody seems to be home."

"He's out of town," Eve replied.

"Oh, that's it...for how long, do you know?"

"Only a couple of days." She paused for a moment, then surprised herself by asking, "Why are you looking for him?"

"I'd like to talk to him about the house and see if he has any plans. Olive said something about wanting to sell it."

He spoke as if Olive were still alive.

Eve looked at him for a moment and thought he was what people referred to as a 'wheeler-dealer'. "Well, I wouldn't know about that," she responded.

"A shame what happened," said Dave, as he scratched his head.

"Yes, it was," added Eve.

"Nice lady too. Sure was sorry to hear about her."

Nice lady? Eve felt her face stiffen and wondered if this man really believed everything he said. She'd met him once before when they first moved to Arizona and had taken an instant disliking to him. A "veritable second garden of childhood," she remembered him calling Sunshine Valley. She told Adam she didn't feel comfortable with the man and thought they should look for another agent to show them around. Adam listened patiently to his wife's objections, then told her he thought it was mostly Dave's profession that she objected to and not him personally. In the end, she acquiesced and it was Dave Wilcox who sold them their home.

"Say, Dave, in all your driving around here, you haven't seen Raul lately, have you?" Eve finally asked.

Dave looked puzzled, as if he didn't know who she was referring to.

"The gardener who works here," she added.

"Oh...him. Nope. Haven't seen him in a long time. I expect he's gone back to Mexico. They do that, you know...come here and work for a few months, make some money, then go back home. He'll be back when the pesos run out."

It was all Eve could do to be civil. Everything seemed to annoy her today, but she forced herself to continue asking questions. "By any chance, did you see him the morning Olive died?"

"Let me see...the morning Olive drowned...I don't remember. I'll think about it, though, and let you know."

"Thanks, Dave. You do that." Eve glared at him and thought, *much more of this and she could really start to dislike Sunshine Valley*. Making her way around the car, she turned to go home, leaving Dave standing with a broad grin on his face.

Chapter 8

Next to painting, studying a foreign language was the best therapy Eve knew to block out unwanted thoughts and images. Once she returned to the safety of her home, she decided to try and free her mind of all negative thoughts by focusing on something more productive. As she picked up her German book and walked out to the patio table, she began conjugating the ten most common verbs. "Ich bin...du bist...sie ist..." Coco looked up and tilted her head, as if to question the meaning of all these new, strange sounds that Eve was making.

Although Eve and Adam had been to Europe several times, they had never visited Germany. Eve was looking forward to the trip and set her mind on learning as much of the language as possible. As far back as she could remember, she had expressed a love for languages. She was always fascinated by the fact that the human voice could make so many different sounds and what might sound like gibberish to one person would be totally comprehensible to someone else. Besides English, she was fluent in French and Spanish. She could also order food in a restaurant, politely ask for directions, and thank people for their help in Italian, Swedish, and Portuguese. She even prided herself on being able to count to ten in both Japanese and Russian. Eve always believed it was essential to be able to communicate with people in their native tongue. They respect you more, she told Adam. Even if you only know a few words, it shows that you care about them and their culture.

How long had Eve been sitting at the table doing her grammar exercises? She had lost all awareness of time and was glad. A tiny drop of water fell on her book and she looked up. Dark clouds were threatening overhead. Although she didn't really want to get up, she decided she'd better, as the intermittent drops turned into a steady sprinkle.

She walked over to the patio wall and wasn't sure why she happened to look across at Frank's house. To her surprise, she noticed that his door was open. Had she forgotten to close it when she went to feed Petticoat? Had Frank returned earlier than expected? *It was probably best to go over there and make certain everything was okay*, she thought. Besides, she'd feel terrible if the cat ran out and got hurt.

Eve left through the patio gate and quickly ran towards her neighbor's house, trying not to get too wet. As she suspected, the back door was open several inches. She pushed it further and listened for signs of Frank's presence. From one of the back rooms, she heard the sound of drawers opening and shutting. Eve felt her heart start to pound. *Get out of here*, something told her, but, this time, she didn't listen to her inner voice. Spurred on by tenacity as much as curiosity, she silently crept towards the rear of the house. *The den*, she thought, *picturing the layout of the house that was similar to hers.*

Whoever it was, the person seemed frantic. As she reached the room, Eve saw the back of a woman who was stooped over the desk, rifling through a stack of papers. A wave of shock ran through her body when she recognized the intruder. "Pearl...is that you? What on earth are you doing here?" she yelled in disbelief.

The woman whirled around in surprise. She hadn't heard Eve enter the room and was struck speechless.

"What are you doing here?" Eve repeated.

Pearl dropped the bundle she was holding in her hands and papers of all sizes began floating to the floor. "Oh, no," she moaned, "what are *you* doing here?"

"I noticed the door was open. I was here earlier and thought I'd forgotten to close it when I came to feed Petticoat...but..."

Pearl didn't allow Eve to finish. "You shouldn't have come in...This is so upsetting," she stammered.

Eve glanced around the room. Obviously, this woman had been searching for something, but hadn't yet found it.

"I think I better go now," Pearl said nervously, as she turned towards the door.

"Wait a minute," said Eve, blocking her path. Two of the desk drawers were half open and several books had been knocked to the floor. Evidently, Pearl had been carrying out her search for some time. "Exactly what is it that you're looking for?" Eve demanded to know.

The woman began to blush. Little drops of perspiration appeared on her forehead. Gripping the edge of the desk, she took a deep breath and slowly began to offer something resembling an explanation. "I've been looking for something that belongs...to me. It's mine," she stammered.

Hesitating and gasping after every few words, Pearl sounded as if she was either going to say something of the utmost importance or simply collapse. Eve was incredulous, as her glance shifted between Pearl and the papers scattered on the floor. Suddenly, she recalled the accusation that Maggie Walsh had made about this woman. Was Pearl really the thief Maggie claimed she was? If so, then she wasn't a very accomplished one.

Because the woman seemed genuinely distraught, Eve took her by the arm and led her to a chair. "I think you better sit down for a minute, Pearl."

"Maybe you're right...I'm so...embarrassed."

"Would you like a glass of water?" Eve asked, softening her voice.

"Yes...maybe I better. I feel so weak."

Eve left the woman who sat shaking in the semi-darkness and rushed into the kitchen. When she returned a few minutes later with a box of tissues and a glass of water, Pearl began to sob uncontrollably.

"Here," coaxed Eve, holding out the glass to the distraught woman, "drink this slowly. It will help calm you down."

"You don't...understand," muttered Pearl between the tears.

"Use this," said Eve, handing her a tissue.

Gradually, Pearl began to regain her composure..

"Would you like to tell me about it?" Eve asked gently. "Perhaps you'll feel better if you tell me why you're here and what you're looking for."

The woman lifted her head and squinted, revealing an expression of deep anguish in her blood shot eyes. Haltingly, she began her explanation. "I'm trying to find something that Olive has...I mean had...about me. I knew nobody was home, so I...finally worked up the nerve to come over here. I know she kept a key under the mat. I found it and I let myself in. I wasn't trying to steal anything. I just want what belongs to me."

"Why don't you tell me what it is that you want to find. Maybe I can help you." Eve felt uneasy about her offer, but the sight of this pitiful woman left her no choice. "But, first, I think you better tell me everything, Pearl."

"Maybe you're right." She blew her nose and wiped her eyes with a handful of tissues.

"Go ahead. I'm listening," urged Eve.

"Well, after my husband died...you never knew him, did you?" Pearl asked. reluctantly.

"No, I never did, but, please, go on. What about your husband?"

Pearl took a deep breath as she continued her confession. "Well, when he died, I was beside myself. We'd been married for over thirty years...He'd been sick in bed for months...heart trouble...I took care of him every day. I took such good care of him...you must believe me, fed him...read to him...everything..."

"I do believe you, Pearl," Eve reassured her.

A look of hope filled the woman's eyes. "One morning," she continued, "I went into the bedroom, as usual, to give him his medicine and found him...he must have passed away...in his sleep...during the night." Her gasps were becoming louder and deeper.

"Slow down. Take your time...there's no hurry." Eve cautioned.

"At first, I was shocked...even though I'd been expecting it...then, little by little, I began to feel some relief...he had suffered so much...you know what I mean?" Pearl begged for support.

"Yes, Pearl. I understand," replied Eve. Although she was trying to console the woman, she felt herself becoming increasingly uncomfortable.

"John always took care of everything. I didn't know what to do when he died...where to turn...so. I just did the simplest things I was capable of doing. I brushed his hair and dressed him in his favorite blue suit...he looked so peaceful." She hesitated for a moment, blew her nose again, then continued. "I sat with him like that for a while...talking to him, holding his hand, and then...I don't know...it was as if he spoke to me...It was as if he was telling me to go ahead and do it."

"Do what?" demanded Eve. "What was he telling you to do?"

"To bury him...in the garden. He always loved his garden. So, I looked around and found Raul and asked him...to dig up the rose bushes and make a hole. He didn't say anything, just started digging and digging...until finally...I thought it was deep enough. I went inside and told John it was ready. I sat down next to him and began reading a passage from the Bible. I played his favorite music...then, with the help of Raul, the two of us carried him out to the garden and buried him in the ground."

Eve was stunned. She looked at Pearl and tried to picture this tiny woman and the gardener carrying a dead man's body out to the patio and burying him.

"We covered him with the dirt and replaced...the rose bushes on top of his grave." She paused for a moment, then began to smile. "I paid Raul and thanked him. He didn't seem to mind all the work. I sat in the patio for a few hours talking to John. Then, I went to bed and had one of the most peaceful nights I'd had in a long time. I felt that everything was going to be okay again, until..." She broke off her sentence and Eve looked at her, uncertain if she'd finished or if she was merely trying to catch her breath.

"Until what? What happened?" Eve asked, when she realized the woman was hesitant to continue.

"I told you that John had always...taken care of everything...bills and anything that had to do with money. What I didn't realize was that the property we owned was in his name. When I went to the bank, I told them John had died, but they wanted to see a death certificate. I didn't have one and I didn't know what to do. So, from then on, I decided to pretend that he was still alive and continued signing his name to anything that required a signature. Nobody knew the difference...or asked any questions. Nobody seemed to care."

Eve stared at the woman in astonishment. It was inconceivable to her that anyone, especially elderly retired people, and particularly this woman, who had a severely ill husband, would be so ignorant about the transfer of property, let alone the reporting of a death. Why hadn't they taken proper steps before John died? Eve knew that many women are at a loss when their husbands die. But this! And what did it have to do with Olive, she wondered? She waited a few moments, trying to regain her composure, then continued to press the distraught woman for more details.

"This is truly an amazing story, Pearl. It must have been very difficult for you. But, I still don't understand what it has to do with Olive and why you are here today."

The woman who, a moment earlier, had been sobbing uncontrollably, heaved a sigh, then found the courage to respond. "After John was gone, I made the mistake of turning to Olive for help. I thought she seemed to know so much and, since she'd had a husband who'd died, I thought she could give me advice...boy, was I wrong."

In spite of the gasping and wheezing, Eve detected a tone of bitterness in Pearl's voice. "What did Olive do?" she asked.

"Well, at first, she pretended she wanted to help. I was so relieved, thinking I'd found someone who could give me good advice. So, I told her everything. What a mistake that was. As soon as I explained to her what I had done, she began yelling at me and calling me a criminal. She said I had broken the law...that I had committed a serious crime...that I could even go to prison for what I had done." Pearl's voice grew louder until she reached a high-pitched whining, then she pulled out another tissue and began to shake again, eyes welling up with tears. "She even suggested that I might have killed John myself and that I probably did it on purpose to get his money. She said...she said...she was...going...to the police. She was going to report me." Once again, Pearl began trembling uncontrollably.

Eve put her arm around the woman's shoulders and began to gently rock her back and forth. How she hated the position in which she found herself! Her aversion to personal revelations was deeply rooted in the conviction that people's private lives should remain that way—private. Pearl continued sobbing and Eve thought that, despite her discomfort, it was time to take control of the situation. "Tell me, Pearl," she asked solemnly, "when did all of this happen?"

"About six months ago," replied Pearl.

"And? What did Olive do? Did she go to the police?"

"No...but, she threatened me every time I saw her. It got so I was afraid to go out of the house. On the day before she died, she told me she'd written a letter saying that I'd...killed my husband. She was going to send it to the police. I was so worried and couldn't sleep all night. The next morning...I saw her leave the house and go to the pool, so I followed her."

Eve stood up abruptly and turned towards Pearl, almost afraid to ask her next question. "What happened that morning? I want you to tell me exactly what you remember." Eve spoke very slowly and seriously.

The clock on the wall began to chime and both women jumped. For a moment, Pearl seemed to lose her train of thought. "What did you say?" she asked weakly.

Eve repeated the question and Pearl stared at her, as if confused by the seriousness in her voice. "I wasn't sure what do to," she responded, "I wanted to talk to her...to beg her not to tell the police. I didn't want to go to jail. I didn't want people coming to the house to dig up John's body."

"Did you talk to her?" demanded Eve.

"No. When I got to the pool, I stopped by the gate and waited. I heard her in there. She was yelling at somebody."

"Who? Who was with her? Who was she yelling at?" Eve insisted.

"I don't know. I never went in. I wanted to see her alone. I didn't want to have to face anyone else."

"What was Olive saying?" Eve looked at Pearl expectantly, waiting to hear more.

"I don't remember. I was so upset."

"Think! Try to remember what you heard." The urgency in Eve's voice intensified.

"I was in a daze. She was screaming about something that had to do with breaking the law and telling the authorities. At first, I thought she was talking about me, but, then I realized she was threatening someone else. She was an evil woman."

"Did you hear anything else? A name? Did Olive call the person she was yelling at by name? Was there anyone else nearby?" Eve was becoming increasingly exasperated.

"I can't remember. I was so scared...so, I just turned around and went home. Later on, I heard that she had drowned. Eve, you can't imagine how relieved I was when I heard the news. I'm so ashamed to say it, but I've never been so glad about..." She broke off and began sobbing again.

Eve finally understood the reason for Pearl's presence in Frank's house. "It's okay Pearl...don't worry. So, that's why you came here. You're looking for the letter Olive claims she wrote."

"Yes...I thought if I could find it...and destroy it before Frank found it...I've never done anything like this before. You must believe me."

Eve started pacing again. Petticoat appeared in the doorway, blinking and looking up with curiosity at the two women. "Did you find anything? Did you find the letter?" she asked.

"No, and I've looked everywhere. I don't know where she could have put it. Maybe she already sent it to the police."

"Well, I doubt it. You would have heard something by now if she had. No, Pearl, I don't think you need to worry. I'm quite sure that there never was a letter. Olive was a malicious woman and I think she enjoyed threatening people whenever she could, but I strongly doubt that she ever wrote a letter about you."

"I hope you're right," Pearl whimpered.

"There's one other thing, Pearl. This is important. When you were standing outside the pool that morning and heard Olive, could you tell if it was a man or a woman that she was yelling at?" Eve's curiosity was heightened by the new revelation, but frustrated by the lack of details.

"I couldn't tell. I don't know...I didn't see anyone."

"So, it could have been a woman?"

"Well...yes...I suppose...I really don't know who it was."

Eve was uncertain about what she should do next, but thought it best to try and get this woman home. "Now, my dear, I think it's time for us to get out of here," she said gently, as she took Pearl's arm.

"Oh, Eve, I'm so glad I could tell you about this. Do you think it will be okay? Do you think I'll have to go to jail? I couldn't bear being locked up." She looked and sounded like a helpless child. Although Eve wanted to reassure her, she wasn't certain what the eventual outcome of all of this turmoil would be. Adam would probably have an answer. *Wait till he hears this incredible story,* she thought.

"Things usually work out for the best," said Eve, hating the noncommittal answer she felt forced to give. "But," she added, "you can't go breaking into people's houses. Come on, let's put everything back the way you found it. I'll help you."

The two women straightened up the room, replacing papers and tidying the desk. When they finished, Eve felt quite certain Frank wouldn't notice that anything was out of place. *In fact,* she thought, *the room was probably neater than the way he had left it.*

Eve led Pearl out of the house and felt relieved to be in the open air, even though they were inundated by a steady stream of rain that came pouring down. *This gloomy weather is certainly appropriate,* she thought, *a perfect reflection of all that has transpired.* The two women ran across the street, awkwardly jumping over little puddles of water that had collected on the pavement.

Once inside her own home, Pearl seemed like a different person. She took a deep breath, then smiled broadly. "I'll be fine now," she said reassuringly, then disappeared into the rear of the house. She left Eve standing in the doorway, shaking off the water from her arms. When Pearl didn't immediately return, she stepped inside.

Eve had always admired the way Pearl furnished her home. From where she was standing, she could see the living room and dining room, and she took the opportunity to survey the contents of both. The rooms were filled with Santa Fe style furniture. A row of Kachina dolls stood on top of a carved shelf, and a multicolored Indian rug highlighted the brown tiled floor. She thought Pearl's taste was very similar to her own.

Although she might have been reluctant to admit it, Eve couldn't help but look around to see if she could spot a green crystal vase. At first, she had dismissed the idea that Pearl could have stolen the vase, but, based on what had just occurred at Frank's house, she was no longer so certain. Considering Pearl's incredible revelation, wasn't anything possible? *Perhaps Maggie Walsh wasn't so wrong after all*, she thought.

Eve saw nothing resembling the green vase that Maggie spoke of, but she couldn't help noticing the group of photographs that were lined up on a small round table in a corner of the living room. She moved closer to get a better look. One picture in particular caught her attention. A handsome man in a Navy uniform, obviously an old photograph, occupied the center of the collection. Picking up the gold frame, she thought how much he reminded her of Adam.

"That's John," explained a voice from behind Eve's back. "He was in the Navy during the war. I love this picture. It's my favorite." Pearl approached Eve, took the photograph from her and smiled broadly as she wiped the glass with her sleeve.

"Yes, it's very nice. I was just admiring it. He looks a little like Adam. He was in the Navy too."

"Here," said Pearl, holding out an umbrella, "I brought you this. I'm afraid it's a little late, but maybe it will help."

Eve accepted the offer and thanked the woman. She was anxious to leave and get back home. Adam would certainly have returned by now and was probably wondering where she was. Besides, she had so much to tell him and couldn't wait to hear his reaction.

"If you need help, Pearl, please don't hesitate to call us." Eve thought she saw a look of sadness in the woman's eyes.

"Yes, I will. Thank you so much," she stammered.

"Well, thank you for the umbrella. I'll return it as soon as I can."

Outside, the pavement was wet and slippery. Eve stepped tentatively, trying to avoid slipping. She had fallen once before, bruising herself badly and she didn't want to repeat the experience. With her eyes focused on the ground, she headed for home and didn't notice Adam who was standing in the doorway, smiling.

"Nice weather for a walk," he called to his wife.

"Oh, Adam," she said with a start. "You scared me."

"Come inside," he said. "I have something exciting to tell you."

So many things seemed to be happening at once and Eve wondered if she could stand any more excitement, but she slowly followed her husband inside.

"I think I've solved the mystery," said Adam, hardly able to control his enthusiasm.

"What?" asked Eve, shocked. "You found out who killed Olive?"

"Olive? Oh, no," he laughed. "But, you better dry yourself first. You're all wet."

He was right. Eve was thoroughly drenched. "What did you solve? Don't keep me in suspense," she pleaded.

"I think I know why the last Zeppelin cover I bought has that unusual Berlin postmark." Adam was radiant. He looked like someone who had made an important scientific discovery that would change the course of mankind. Had she not been so wet, Eve would have put her arms around her husband and hugged him. Instead, she went into the kitchen, took a towel from a cabinet, and began to dry herself.

"I want you to tell me all about it, my dear," she said, shaking the water from her hair.

For the next two hours, Adam recounted the details of his discovery. Eve listened, as if mesmerized, and marveled at the fact that a grown man, and an intelligent one at that, could become so passionate about little pieces of paper. Although she didn't share her husband's obsession, this time, she welcomed it and found comfort in the innocence of it all.

Eve wondered how she was going to tell Adam about her day. She didn't have the heart to spoil his pleasure. *Later*, she thought, *after dinner*. However, most of the evening was filled with a discussion about stamps and the trip to Germany that they were planning. As the evening wore on, it seemed to Eve that Adam had said everything he wanted to say about his research project. *Finally,* she thought, *it's time*. She turned to her husband and asked, "Do you ever think about how easy it is for someone to commit a crime...and get away with it?"

Not waiting for a response, Eve began to tell Adam about her day and how she had found Pearl rifling through the drawers in Frank's house. She recounted the details of the death of Pearl's husband, the burial of his body in the garden, and Olive's threat to inform the police.

Chapter 9

Had Adam Iverson not respected his wife's judgment as much as he did, he might have simply attributed her suspicions to an overly active imagination. But, as he'd learned so many times over the years, it was wise to give credence to her feelings. Within minutes, Eve was able to assess every new situation or person she encountered and her opinions were usually correct. So, when Eve began to recount all the events of the day and what conclusions she had drawn, Adam listened attentively.

"The point is, I'm more certain than ever that Olive's demise was not an accident. Even though Valium was found in her body, I don't think it had anything to do with her death. I know Frank thinks he unintentionally killed his wife by slipping her the tranquilizer. However, it appears that he'd been putting the medication in her coffee for quite a while and my guess is that she had probably developed some immunity to it. No, I'm convinced that she was murdered by someone, and the murder was not accidental, but deliberate. Someone, for some reason, wanted her gone." Her voice was soft, but emphatic.

"If you're right, and you usually are," Adam replied in a calm, but serious tone, "I think it might be a bit dangerous for you to stir things up. Let somebody else handle the situation. You don't need this...certainly not now. You're supposed to be retired, remember? Perhaps you should talk to the police and tell them what you suspect."

"The police?" Eve said scornfully. "You mean that poor, helpless deputy Bud Warner who has trouble writing a speeding ticket? No, thank you. I got the distinct impression that he was only mildly interested in Olive's death. Besides, it's still all conjecture. I doubt that anyone would believe me since I don't have actual proof of anything...at least not yet."

"Yet? What do you intend to do next? I certainly hope you're not planning on becoming more involved in this mess." Adam was growing increasingly apprehensive about the direction of Eve's plans.

"I'm not sure what to do next, but I really wish I could find Raul. I have a strong feeling he might have some answers. Nobody has seen him for more than a week. I wonder...You were friendly with him. Do you think it's possible that he could have killed Olive?"

Adam hesitated for a moment, not quite certain how to respond to Eve's question. "I don't know," he began slowly, "I guess anything's possible, but somehow I doubt it. He seemed like a quiet man and never struck me as someone who had a bad temper. I never had any unpleasant encounters with him...actually, just the opposite."

"Oh, Adam," sighed Eve, "I seem to be getting more suspicious the older I get. I'm beginning to think anyone is capable of committing a crime and, as I've sadly learned, so are we."

Adam looked at Eve in astonishment. "What do you mean? I certainly haven't committed any crimes, at least none that I know of...have you? Do you have a confession you want to make?"

"Well, I did take the opportunity to spy on Pearl Thomas when I went to her house. I didn't see Maggie's vase, but who knows? I glanced around a couple of rooms, but wasn't able to look very carefully. Of course, she could have hidden it somewhere.

Perhaps spying isn't exactly what you'd call a crime, but I still don't think it's very nice, and I'm not particularly proud of myself."

"Is that all that's bothering you?" Adam replied, trying to stifle a laugh.

"That, and something a little more serious... something that concerns you. I'm disturbed by the fact that Frank told you he gave his wife Valium and you never said anything about it to me or to the authorities. What worries me is that, if, by some chance, Olive's death were to be attributed to her husband, your guilty knowledge and subsequent silence could be interpreted as aiding and abetting. I'd hate to see you get into trouble simply because you were trying to be a good friend."

Adam was at a loss to respond, as Eve continued. "I also know that Pearl buried her husband in the garden and has been forging his name on legal documents for over a year. For all we know, she could have killed him as well. Now, like you, I have guilty knowledge about a crime. I'm afraid we both know more than we should and that we're getting caught up in some very sordid business here in paradise. Not all the people who live in Sunshine Valley are exactly what they appear to be."

"Don't worry, Eve. You're a long way from becoming a criminal. Anyway, I'll stop you when I think you're getting out of hand. I don't think you need to worry about what Pearl told you. If it makes you feel any better, I'll talk to her and see if we can help straighten out this mess. She really does need to report her husband's death to the proper authorities."

"Oh, Adam, would you? That would be wonderful. She can't go on forging her husband's name forever. I didn't say anything to her, but she really could get in some serious trouble for that little caper."

Eve was grateful that Adam had volunteered to help Pearl. She was going to ask him, but was glad he spared her having to make the request. Actually, she was surprised Adam didn't find Pearl's behavior unusual. He had seen it at the hospital before, he explained, widows who were at a complete loss after the death of their husbands. They weren't sure what to do with all the complicated paperwork. Perhaps Pearl's actions were a little unorthodox, but it didn't really surprise him.

"Did you ever meet her husband?" Eve asked.

"No. Actually, I thought she was a single gal."

"Well, she is now."

Although Eve was still bothered by the fact that somebody had accused her and Adam of having killed Olive, she couldn't bring herself to tell him about that piece of gossip too, at least not now. She knew he'd be upset and what little energy she had left was slowly draining out of her. Overcome by fatigue, she went to bed early. However, in spite of her exhaustion, she spent another restless night, mentally reviewing all the events and impressions of the past week. She had a gnawing feeling that she was forgetting something important, but, eventually managed to drift off into a light sleep.

The next morning, Adam awakened earlier than usual. During the night, he had decided to use Coco as an excuse to do some investigating of his own, partly because of what Eve had told him and partly because he wanted to help Frank. In reality, however, a battle of wits was developing between Adam and his wife. They both sensed it, but, to maintain the peace, neither of them was willing to openly acknowledge it.

Because the pool seemed to be the logical place to apply his deductive skills, Adam decided to make it his first stop. "Come on, Coco. Let's see what's happening out there." The dog looked up at him as if uncertain about the invitation. But, when Adam reached for the leash, she began jumping up and barking excitedly.

Since animals were not allowed in the pool area itself, Adam stayed along the outside edge. Now and then, Coco stopped to sniff a flower. What was it he hoped to find? He wasn't exactly sure, but following his wife's hunch, he too thought the key to the mystery might be hidden somewhere within these walls. After a while, he started to feel self conscious and decided to return home. Glancing across the street, he noticed Harry Wells who was coming out of his house. He waved and walked over to talk to him.

"Morning, Harry. How's it going? Any luck with the house?" Adam asked.

The man was carrying a bag of garbage and stopped for a second to acknowledge Adam's greeting before continuing to the curb. "Not yet," he replied, depositing the bag in the underground container.

"You'll sell it. The right person will come along. You'll see. It's just a matter of time," Adam assured him.

"I was sure we had some buyers last week...a couple from Illinois. Dave Wilcox told me they loved the house, but, it seems everything fell through. Just goes to show you, though, it's not sold till it's sold."

"What happened?" asked Adam.

"Beats me. Nice couple too. Dave brought them here three times. He said they were ready to make an offer...but, so much for empty promises."

"Well, they might still come back."

"I doubt it. I have a hunch they got scared off. It's that darned woman's fault."

"Who's that?" asked Adam.

"Olive Howell...her drowning in the pool probably scared them off. They were here that morning. Darned woman. She always did cause trouble, alive or dead."

Adam saw an opening and took it. "Say, you didn't happen to notice anything, did you?" he asked.

"What do you mean?" Harry looked puzzled.

"That morning," continued Adam, "did you see Olive, or Raul, or anything unusual?"

"Me? No. I wasn't even here. I thought it would be better if the couple could look around by themselves, so Mary and I left early. She had some shopping to do, so we drove into Tucson for the day. When we came back, the sheriff was already here and a crowd had gathered by the pool."

Adam frowned and hoped his disappointment wasn't too obvious. "Well, Harry," he said, "I'm sure you'll have better luck next time. It won't take long. These places usually go pretty fast and you have one of the best."

"I hope you're right," replied Harry. After a few seconds, he looked squarely at Adam. "Say, you're the one who found her..."

"Yes. Eve and I found her...she was in the Jacuzzi." Adam replied solemnly.

"Must have been quite a shock for the two of you...but it's too bad she picked that morning to go and drown."

"Did Dave tell you if he saw anything—anything strange?" continued Adam.

"No, not a word. If he did see something odd, he didn't tell me about it. He was just as disappointed as I was to lose the sale though. He thought for sure that the man and woman were going to make an offer. I don't know what to think. People are funny about this kind of thing. Probably thought Olive's death was an omen or something."

"Well, once everything settles down, and people forget about Olive's drowning, you'll have a buyer," said Adam, trying to provide more words of encouragement.

"I hope that happens soon. I've never seen so many people at the pool as I have this week. I don't know what folks expect to find."

Adam hoped his neighbor didn't include him among the curiosity-seekers and tried to assume an air of detachment. "Everything will get back to normal soon," he repeated calmly.

"We'll see. Well, I'm on my way to the store, "said Harry. "Mary's baking and ran out of butter."

The man got into his car, leaving Adam standing on the sidewalk. He felt he'd made no progress. *Perhaps Eve was mistaken*, he thought. After all, nothing seemed to indicate that Olive's death was anything more than what the official report had said it was—an accident. As was his custom, Adam began to re-examine everything he'd learned, piece by piece, in a very logical manner. Even if Pearl had heard Olive threatening someone, that was nothing new. She picked on everybody and people were used to it. They simply ignored her. As far as the slippers were concerned, it's possible she put them by the Jacuzzi herself. He knew very well how people's habits change, especially women's habits. Perhaps she was upset or distracted. He remembered how cold it had been that morning. Perhaps Olive didn't want to walk barefoot from the Jacuzzi back to the guest book. *No*, decided Adam, logically, there was nothing to indicate anything out of the ordinary. He did wish, however, that Eve might be right. As much as he hated to admit it, he knew Frank's guilt would be assuaged if someone actually had murdered his wife.

When Adam returned home, he found Eve busy packing. She was in the bedroom filling two large boxes with old clothes and shoes that she'd promised to bring to the Lions Club for their rummage sale.

"Where have you two been this morning?" she asked when Adam entered the house.

"We went for a little walk," Adam answered cautiously.

"To the pool?"

"Are you part bloodhound?" Adam responded jokingly.

"What's that supposed to mean? I simply asked if you went to the pool," replied Eve curtly.

"We went there...at least we walked around the outside since they don't allow dogs inside, but we went other places as well."

"That's nice." Eve continued packing, ignoring her husband's awkwardness.

"I ran into Harry Wells," admitted Adam.

As much as Eve would have liked to ignore her husband's sarcasm, she was too curious to hear what he might have discovered. "What did he say? Does he know anything? Did he see something?" she asked eagerly.

"No, I'm afraid not. It seems he wasn't even home when Olive drowned. He and his wife were in Tucson."

Eve's interest turned to disappointment. "Darn! So, he didn't see anything either. Nobody seems to have seen anything."

"Harry thought he'd sold the house, but Olive's death appears to have scared away the potential buyers."

"Was that the couple we saw coming out of the house?" asked Eve.

"Apparently. Dave told Harry they were ready to make an offer too...but, the deal fell through."

Eve returned to her packing. When she finished filling two cardboard boxes, she asked Adam to help her carry them to the car. "It's amazing how much junk we accumulate. I thought we'd gotten rid of everything when we moved here," she sighed as she lifted the end of one box.

"I hope you're not giving away anything good." Adam looked fondly at the two brown cartons they'd carefully placed in the car.

"You won't miss a thin   I assure you," responded Eve, as she closed the trunk before her husband had a chance to question her further.

"Will you be gone long?" asked Adam.

"Not too long. I'm going to drop off these clothes, then I'm going to swing by Sunshine Gallery to see if they've sold either of my paintings. That's it...I'm not going anywhere else."

"Take your time," said Adam. "I need to sort through the notes I took yesterday."

Before Adam had a chance to say anything more, Eve slid behind the wheel. Backing out of the driveway, she waved to her husband and headed straight for the Lions Club. When she arrived, she went around back to the door marked "Donations," asked one of the attendants to help her remove the boxes from the trunk, got her receipt, then returned to her car and made her way to the art gallery.

Since it was a particularly clear and mild day, Eve rolled down the two front windows. She could really get used to days like these, she thought, as she inhaled the fragrant air. Nowhere had she ever seen such magnificent blue skies or billowy white clouds. All around, mountains loomed toward the sky and every detail of the rugged landscape was intensified by the bright sunlight.

Sunshine Gallery was located in a medium-sized shopping complex at the edge of town. Eve drove in and found an empty parking space directly in front of the small building. As she got out of the car, she looked up admiringly at the display of paintings in the window. Some were abstract, but they all depicted different interpretations of the desert. *Looks like Jack is getting ready for a new exhibit*, she thought.

The owner of the gallery, Jack Slater, was also an artist. He had opened a studio several years before, as a venue for his own paintings. But, as Sunshine Valley continued to grow, he decided to expand his business and display the work of other artists as well as his own. When Adam learned of the gallery, he brought some of Eve's paintings to show Jack who immediately suggested including two of them in an upcoming show.

Eve had been present at the opening of her exhibit several weeks earlier. This was a new experience for her and one which she thoroughly enjoyed. However, even though her paintings drew a good deal of attention, it didn't really matter to her how other people judged them. What gave her the greatest sense of satisfaction was the personal sense of creativity she experienced when arranging shapes and colors on a blank canvas.

One of Eve's biggest problems was that, once she finished a painting, she was reluctant to part with it. But, in a sensible moment, she realized, there just wasn't enough room in the house for all her work. Most of the walls were already covered with her canvases and she was running out of space in which to store the others.

Now, as she walked up the ramp that led to the gallery, she pulled open the heavy door and entered, curious to learn the status of her precious *objets d'art*.

Because it was still early, she didn't see anyone in the two main rooms.

"Mrs. Iverson, I'm so glad you're here. I was getting ready to call you." A tall man wearing a cowboy shirt, blue jeans, and boots emerged from a back room and smiled broadly at Eve.

"Well, I beat you to it." Eve looked at the man and smiled. *If only Adam could see this*, she thought. He would love what Jack was wearing. "I was just passing by and thought I'd stop in and see if we've had any luck."

As Eve waited for the man to reply, his smile slowly disappeared. "I'm afraid I have some bad news for you."

"What is it, Jack?" asked Eve, cheerfully, "No takers?"

"Well, it's not that," the man responded in a somber voice. "I really hate to have to tell you this, but I'm afraid one of your paintings has been stolen."

"You're kidding! Are you serious?" This was certainly not something Eve expected to hear.

"Yes, I'm afraid so. Although quite a few people admired them, nobody made an offer. Since I'm installing a new exhibit, I took down your two paintings a couple of days ago. I put them in the storeroom myself. Then, yesterday, I went to call you to let you know that you could come and pick them up, but I noticed that one was missing. I thought maybe I'd misplaced it, but I looked everywhere and couldn't find it. I'm usually here all alone and try to keep a watchful eye on everything, but this does happen occasionally. Since this is your first experience with the gallery, I'm so sorry it had to happen to you."

"Well, at least we know that somebody wanted it," said Eve, at a loss for what to say.

"One good thing, however," the man replied, "we're insured for theft and I have a check for you." He walked back behind a counter and brought out an envelop. "It's for three hundred dollars. That's the price of the painting, less commission. Please...take it," he said as he handed the envelop to Eve. "I called my insurance company and explained what happened. I'll be reimbursed for the loss."

"Are you sure?" she asked, reluctantly.

"Absolutely...Just think of it as a sale. It's just that you don't know who the new owner is." They both laughed.

After some conversation about the possibility of exhibiting more paintings in the future, Eve picked up her one remaining canvas and returned to the car. She slid the painting into the back seat, then got behind the wheel and switched on the engine. *Well*, she thought, *another new experience*. I wonder how many more are in store for me in this seemingly quiet little town. She shook her head and smiled, a bit perplexed, but somewhat amused by what had just happened. She made her way down the main road, then turned left onto Camino Avion.

As Eve drove down the street, she happened to notice a man raking the ground between two houses. Was it Raul? She'd passed by too quickly to get a good look, so she backed up and pulled the car over to the curb. After she got out, she walked back to the pathway. Her footsteps made a crunching sound as she made her way across the gravel. Lying on the ground was a pile of dead cactus and some branches, but nothing else. Where did he go? She was certain she'd seen someone raking leaves only a moment ago. Suddenly, she heard little scraping noises coming from around the corner of one of the houses. She walked down to the arroyo and saw the back of the gardener.

"Raul," she called out, "is that you?"

The man continued digging, ignoring her question. She inched closer, certain she'd found the man she had been so eager to locate. When she came within a few inches of the stooped figure, he stopped what he was doing and turned to look at her. It wasn't Raul. It was someone else, someone she didn't recognize.

"Oh, excuse me," said Eve, apologetically, as she backed away. "I thought for a minute that you were Raul."

The man wiped his forehead and stared at her blankly.

"Where's Raul? Donde esta Raul?" Eve asked.

"Raul? No...se fue...gone," he said haltingly.

"Do you know where he is?" Eve asked him in Spanish.

"No...se fue," the man repeated.

"Gracias." Eve turned and walked back to her car. Now, she was more eager than ever to locate Raul. He had to know something. She was certain that was the explanation for his disappearance. He had probably seen or heard the killer and was afraid to come forward. It bothered her that none of the residents of Sunshine Valley seemed to notice, or even care, that he was missing. She caught herself. It was unlike her to be annoyed at so many things. Perhaps she and Adam should have stayed in California after all, she reflected. Despite the fact that she found the Arizona desert beautiful, she hated the restlessness and disturbing thoughts that she'd been experiencing the past few days.

As she pulled into the driveway of her house, Eve saw Tom Wicks approaching her mailbox. *If anyone had seen Raul, it would be the mailman,* thought Eve.

"Hello, Tom," she said smiling.

"Morning...out for an early spin?" he asked.

"I had to drop some things off at the Lions Club and then stop in at my gallery...just a few errands...nothing terribly exciting. Say, Tom...you haven't seen Raul anywhere, have you?

"Raul?" he asked quizzically.

"The gardener." She tried to control her impatience.

"I know who you mean, but I can't say as I've seen him lately. These fellows come and go, you know, not like..."

"Yes...yes, I know." Eve didn't let him finish.

"Probably back in Mexico by now," he added.

"Do you remember...about a week ago, when Adam and I were on our way to the pool? We saw you..." Eve was certain Tom would have some valuable knowledge.

"Do you mean the day Olive Howell drowned?" he asked.

"Yes, that's the morning I mean." She felt an urgent need to speed up the conversation, a need not shared by the mailman.

"Yeah. I remember. Seems like that's all anybody talks about these days," he drawled.

"You didn't happen to notice anything, did you?" she asked quickly.

"Notice anything? Like what?" The man appeared confused by her question.

"Did you see or hear anything unusual that morning...anything out of the ordinary?" Eve's voice took on an urgent tone as she pressed Tom for more information.

Tom scratched his head and thought for a moment. "Nothing out of the ordinary. I heard Olive yelling at someone in the pool, if you can call that unusual."

"Did you hear what she was saying?" *Now we're getting somewhere,* thought Eve.

"No. I didn't pay much attention...just yelling like she always did. It didn't seem any different from what I'd heard before and I usually would tune out."

"Did you see anyone? Did you see who she was yelling at?" pressed Eve.

"I don't know...I'm not sure..." he answered reluctantly.

"Try to remember who you saw that morning, Tom." Eve was convinced the man had more information and wanted to shake it out of him.

"Wait...I remember now...I saw Raul. Yes, come to think of it. He didn't have a truck that morning. I know he shares one with another gardener...That's the last time I saw him, now that you mention it. He's probably the person Olive was yelling at...she was always after him about something."

"Did you see anybody else?" Eve asked quickly, before he lost his train of thought. "Think," she urged, when there was no reply. "Maybe you saw someone else..."

"Well, I saw Dave Wilcox. I stopped to talk to him. He was waiting to show Harry Wells' house to some folks. I saw Pearl Thomas, too. She took one look at me, then turned her head...I'm not that bad looking, am I?"

"Well," Eve answered abruptly, "a shave wouldn't hurt," then continued her interrogation. "So, that's all you saw? Are you sure?"

"That's all I remember," responded the man, rubbing the stubble on his chin with his right hand.

"Did you see Paula and Doty...the Irish sisters?" continued Eve.

"Oh, yes...that's right. At least I saw one of them...Doty, I think."

"They weren't together? Are you sure you didn't see both of them?" Eve asked with heightened interest.

"Nope, Doty was by herself," the mailman replied, still rubbing his chin. "But, I couldn't tell if she was coming or going. I didn't think it was important and didn't pay much attention."

How odd, thought Eve. She recalled Doty telling her that she and Paula had left the pool together. This was a new revelation and she wondered if it was true or if Tom was mistaken. She thanked him for his help, then turned to go inside before he could ask why she wanted to know so much. Eve found the new information the mailman had provided very interesting and was eager to share it with Adam.

"I'm back," she called out to her husband as she opened the front door. But, there was no reply. "A good watchdog you are," she said to Coco who was busy chewing on a rubber toy in the middle of the living room floor.

Eve made her way into the den, only to find that it too was empty. There was no sign of her husband. The same was true of the rest of the house. She went out to the patio, thinking Adam might be watering the flowers, but he wasn't there either. *Where could he be?* she wondered. She hadn't been gone very long, or had she lost track of time? Looking at her watch, she suddenly realized it was time to feed Petticoat. She'd have to wait until later to tell Adam what she'd discovered.

Eve left through the patio since it was the quickest way to get to Frank's house. Here she was, a retiree, and yet, she'd never been busier. *How had she managed everything when she worked?*, she wondered. At least, then, there was some order in her life. Now, things were out of her control and seemed to be happening so quickly. Lately, her days were filled from early morning until late at night and she found it impossible to finish everything she planned to do.

As she crossed the pathway, Eve looked up and saw Frank's back door standing wide open. *Not again*, she lamented. Hadn't she settled things with Pearl once and for all? She didn't know if she had the energy to repeat another unpleasant scene. As she stood under the arched doorway, Eve heard voices coming from inside the house. She breathed a sigh of relief when she recognized Adam's familiar deep tones. She knocked gently, then pushed open the door and entered.

"Hello," she called out, "it's only me."

She walked into the living room and saw her husband who appeared to be deeply involved in a conversation with Frank. The two men stopped talking, then turned and smiled as Eve entered. "So, there you are!" she said. "I wondered where you'd gone."

"Hello, Eve." Frank was the first to speak. He seemed to be in an unusually good mood.

"Frank came back early," Adam added, sensing his wife's need for an explanation.

"I want to thank you for taking care of Petticoat. I hope she wasn't too much of a bother." Frank leaned over the couch and scooped up the cat in his arms.

"Of course not...no bother at all. She's a sweetheart. We had a great time together."

"Maybe a little finicky about her food, but otherwise, she's pretty good," added Frank.

The cat started purring and he answered her back. It was obvious they were both happy to see each other again.

"Well," Adam said reassuringly, "you let us know if there's anything you need or want."

"I will...and thank you both for all your help," replied Frank.

Eve was struck by the tone of cheerfulness in Frank's voice. It was as if he'd been relieved of a heavy burden. This was a very different man than the one she'd seen a few days earlier, someone so overcome with grief and remorse.

"How did Frank seem to you?" Eve asked Adam once they were home.

"Relieved, I'd say."

"I thought he seemed surprisingly happy for a man whose wife had just died...especially under the circumstances."

Adam ignored the comment. He walked over to a small table and began fingering a row of pipes. Finally, he chose the one he wanted and began to fill it.

"Do you want to tell me what's bothering you, or, do I have to wait?" Eve asked after a few moments.

"I don't know what you're talking about," replied her husband.

"Oh, stop it! I think I know you by now. You always start smoking your pipe when you're worried about something."

"I hadn't noticed."

"Really? Well, it's a little habit of yours that *I* happened to notice over the past forty years or so."

Ignoring his wife's comments, Adam sat down in a chair and began to puff on his pipe.

"Let me ask you something," began Eve, cautiously.

"Anything, my dear."

"What would you do if you thought you'd accidentally killed me?"

Not saying a word, Adam simply paused and blew a puff of smoke into the air.

"You're not answering my question," persisted Eve.

"It's not a fair question," responded Adam.

"Well, then, let me put it another way. How long do you think a man in his late sixties might mourn the loss of a wife he thinks he just killed?"

"I know what you're getting at, but, as we both know, Frank didn't exactly love Olive."

"Precisely. That's my point. Not loving her is one thing, but hating her enough to want her dead...even kill her...is another."

Adam stopped puffing. "But, Frank was at the golf course when Olive drowned," he protested.

"So he was, but maybe he had an accomplice, maybe someone finished the job he started," Eve countered.

"That's preposterous...You know, I think we should put all this unpleasantness aside for now. It's been too much." Then, quickly changing the subject, Adam began to ask Eve about her paintings. "Did you have any luck? Did somebody buy one?"

"Next best thing," replied Eve. "Somebody stole one."

"Don't tell me...You're not serious...Are you telling me the truth?" Adam began puffing on his pipe again.

"Yes, it's true, but it's okay. I'm not upset. At least now I know that somebody wanted one of my paintings...and I got paid for it too," she said, waving the envelope in the air. "Suppose you could say I'm now in the same league with Picasso, Rembrandt, Matisse, and all the other artists whose paintings have been stolen."

Eve was about to tell Adam about her encounter with the gardener when the phone began to ring. She went into the kitchen to answer it. The breathless voice at the other end was barely audible. "It's Doty...could you come over right away? I need to talk to you. It's important."

Chapter 10

Eve was certain that Doty and Paula were concealing something. Now, perhaps she'd have the opportunity to find out what it was they were hiding. As she approached their house, Doty was standing in the open doorway, waiting for her. Shifting her weight from left to right foot, she seemed impatient and smiled broadly when she spotted Eve.

"Thank you for coming so quickly," she called out.

"I got here as fast as I could, but I'm afraid I can't run the way I used to." Eve stopped to catch her breath, then asked, "Has something happened? Is something wrong?"

"Quickly...come inside. Paula's at the store. I need to talk to you before she gets back." Doty took Eve by the hand and pulled her into the house.

So, that was the reason for the urgency, thought Eve. Doty had something to say that she didn't want her companion to know about. More secrets.

"You sounded upset when you called me. Please...tell me what's bothering you," said Eve, getting straight to the point. There was no time for the usual superficial polite exchanges.

"I'm so glad you're here. This is not easy for me, but I felt I had to talk to you...and I really would rather Paula not hear what I have to say...I'm afraid I wasn't completely honest with you this morning." The woman began to fidget nervously with her apron.

Eve recalled what the mailman had said about seeing Doty leave the pool alone and she began to mull over a new idea. She'd never seriously considered the possibility that Olive's killer might be female. *But, after all,* she thought, *if Olive was already sitting in the Jacuzzi, it wouldn't take much strength for a woman to push her head under water and hold it there until she drowned.* Maybe she and Doty had gotten into a fight and Doty pushed her into the water. Eve had often seen her neighbor move heavy furniture with relative ease and she was certainly much stronger than a lot of women her age. She thought Doty could have easily overpowered Olive, especially if she was taken by surprise. Eve's mind began to race. So many new possibilities were popping up, but, she had to admit, none of them were pleasant.

"First of all," began Doty in a very serious low tone, "I'd like to ask you a few questions, if you don't mind."

This was unexpected. Eve had not anticipated the aggressiveness of her neighbor. Alone, she seemed like a different person. She wasn't at all the reticent creature she appeared to be when Paula was present.

"Go ahead. I'll do my best, but I don't know if I'll be able to answer them," Eve responded cautiously.

"Well, there's one thing that's been bothering me," she began. "I really don't understand why you're taking such an interest in Olive's death."

Stunned by the woman's pointed remark, it took Eve a moment before she was able to respond. "I don't know that I'm taking an unusual interest...I'm just a little curious about a few things..." She began searching for something plausible, yet noncommittal, to explain her actions.

"Didn't the coroner say her death was an accident?" Doty's voice was strained.

"Yes, he did," replied Eve.

"You don't think it was anything but an accident, do you?" Doty stared intently at her neighbor, waiting to hear an answer that would relieve her fears. Eve realized there was only one possible answer she could give the distraught woman that would satisfy her. How she hated to lie again! But, there was no choice at this point.

"No, Doty. As far as I know, and, based on the official report, Olive's death appears to have been an accident...that's all I can go by...I haven't heard anything to the contrary." Eve wondered if Doty could sense the lack of sincerity on her voice. Or, did it really matter? Even if the woman knew she was being less than forthright, it was the answer she wanted and desperately needed to hear. Doty took a deep breath and smiled broadly at Eve. The lie had worked.

"Well, then, perhaps I shouldn't have called you after all. I thought maybe you knew something that hadn't been reported, but I guess I was wrong." Doty was beginning to regain her composure.

"Please...I think you should tell me what's really on your mind. Is there something you would just like to let out? You said you weren't completely honest with me this morning. Did you see something you neglected to mention before? Is there something you're holding back?" Eve was persistent. Now that she had the opportunity, she wasn't going to let Doty off the hook too easily. Eve was certain the woman was still concealing something and, like it or not, she was determined to find out what possible bearing the woman's secret might have on Olive's death.

Slowly, Doty began to respond to Eve's questions. "Do you remember how I told you that sometimes I forget things?" She looked at Eve, hoping to find some reassurance.

"Yes, you did," replied Eve. "Go on...tell me what it is that you forgot."

"Well...the morning Olive died, after Paula and I were finished with everything, we left the pool and started to go home. We hadn't gone very far when I realized I'd forgotten my hairbrush...I left it in the dressing room. Paula continued on towards home, but I went back to look for the brush. When I started to open the pool gate, I heard Olive. I opened it quietly, hoping she wouldn't see me. Fortunately, her back was turned. She was standing by the little shed, yelling at Raul."

"Raul?" Eve asked in surprise. Are you sure it was him she was yelling at?"

"Absolutely. I saw the two of them standing there...as plain as day."

"All right. Go on. What happened next?" Eve urged.

"Olive said he was lazy and no good and that he should be ashamed of himself. She claimed he hadn't finished some work he'd started in her patio, so he should hurry up and come over to her house later that morning. He didn't say a word, but I tell you, he was angry. I don't blame him none, either. You should have heard the way she talked to him. And the way he looked at her! I tell you, I got scared myself. If looks could kill...you know what I mean?"

"Did Olive say anything else?" Eve was eager to hear more. *So far,* she thought, *Doty hadn't told her anything new.*

"Anything else? What do you mean?" Doty began to shake.

"Did Olive say anything about Raul being here illegally?"

"I don't think so, not that day, anyway," stammered the woman, "nothing...at least nothing I heard or that I remember I was in a hurry and just wanted to get my brush and get out of there."

"I don't want to put words in your mouth, but didn't Olive say she was going to turn Raul in to the authorities? Report him for being here illegally?" For a moment, Eve was afraid she was revealing too much, but she was determined to find out everything this woman knew.

Doty stared at Eve, her face a blank. She wasn't quite sure how to answer the question. "I never heard her say anything about Raul being here illegally. I just heard her criticizing him for being lazy. He didn't say one word. He just looked past me, then turned and went out. I don't know...maybe he wanted to say something to me, but he didn't."

"And Olive? Did she see you?" Eve pressed Doty for more details.

"Yes. She asked me what I was staring at. I told her I was looking for my brush. When I went into the dressing room, I saw that it was still on the counter, so I grabbed it and got out of there as fast as I could. I sure didn't want to get into a fight with that woman."

Eve was perplexed. Doty's version of what Olive said to Raul didn't seem to coincide with the account she'd heard from Pearl who maintained that Olive was scolding the gardener for being in the country illegally. *Was Doty still trying to conceal something,* she wondered, *or was Pearl mistaken?*

"Tell me, Doty...now, think carefully...as far as you can remember, was Olive wearing her slippers when all this happened?"

"I'm not one hundred percent sure, but I think so. I really didn't look at her that carefully, but I know she was still wearing her robe, so she probably still had her slippers on as well...but I can't say for sure. It all seems kind of hazy to me now."

"Did you see where Raul went when he left?" Eve continued to pressure the woman for more answers.

"He was working by the pool wall...outside. I saw him when I was leaving. I think he was trying to avoid

Olive, or maybe..." She broke off in mid sentence, reluctant to finish her thought. "Eve, do you think Raul could have killed Olive?" she asked after a moment. Doty seemed to brighten at her own suggestion. Apparently, it was a possibility she hadn't considered before.

"At this point, we don't know that Olive was killed by anyone. Remember, as I said before, so far, her death is still regarded as accidental." Eve felt some caution was required. She didn't want to arouse any suspicions in Doty or stir up unwarranted anxiety. After all, she still didn't have a clear idea as to who might have killed Olive, let alone why someone might have felt she deserved to die.

"I know that's what they say, but, I have a feeling you don't believe it...do you?" Doty's voice was becoming increasingly serious.

"At this point, what I think is that we need to find Raul. I'm quite sure he'll be able to shed some light on this whole matter." Eve thought her response appropriately tactful and noncommittal.

"Yes, you're probably right. It's really rather terrible, isn't it? All these suspicions?"

On that point, Eve had to agree. *But,* she wondered, *what suspicions was Doty referring to?* Did she have doubts about someone else that she was not yet prepared to share? Then, she realized what suspicions Doty was referring to. "Oh...now, I understand what's bothering you. You're afraid people might assume that Frank killed his wife. I don't think you need to worry, though. Frank was at the golf course when Olive died...that's where Adam found him...so, you see, he didn't have the opportunity." Eve felt it necessary to provide as much reassurance as possible to her distraught neighbor.

A look of relief spread over the woman's face. "Yes, because of the way Olive treated him, I'm afraid people will presume Frank did it," Doty reluctantly replied, "but, I just knew if anyone would understand, you would."

It was as Eve had suspected. The woman feared that, somehow, Frank might be responsible for his wife's death. She wondered if Doty knew anything about the Valium he had given Olive, but, not wanting to alarm her any further, decided it was best to avoid that topic.

"Is there anything else that's bothering you, Doty?" Eve felt her time was limited since Paula would be returning shortly and she was anxious to find out as much as possible from the neighbor who'd started to open up. She made several attempts to further engage Doty in conversation.

"You know, I'm afraid Paula and I don't have a lot of money..."

Eve wondered what the lack of finances had to do with Olive or Frank. "Yes," she replied softly. "That's true of a lot of retired people. I know it's hard to live on a fixed income...but, you do have a comfortable home."

"Oh, we get by all right, mind you. Don't get me wrong. I'm not complaining, even though there are some things Paula and I have to do without. I keep telling myself we have it better than a lot of folks...and then there's Frank. He's always been so kind to us. From the moment we met him, I knew he was a sweet man. He even offered to buy a hearing aid for Paula. She doesn't know yet. It's a surprise, so don't say anything."

"I won't," Eve reassured her. She glanced over at the vase filled with roses and the implications of Olive's death became clearer. Without her in the picture, a new and happier life was possible for several people. For Frank, there was no longer any need to hide things or sneak out of the house to spend time with Doty and Paula. No more lies or excuses were necessary. Everything seemed to indicate that, finally free of Olive's chains, he had found a more suitable companion with whom he could share his life. What did it matter if this companion also had a companion—or sister? Eve was never sure about Paula and Doty's relationship, but chose not to dwell on it. *In any case,* she thought, *from what she was able to gather, it appeared that this mild-mannered man was quite content to take on both of the women and they, in return, were happy to share him.* Of course, Eve realized in a flash, that's it! That was what she'd sensed in Frank, that twinkle in his eyes that she hadn't seen before. Now, the reason was clear. He was looking forward to his new found freedom and the chance to spend time with Doty and Paula without having to suffer any consequences.

"I'm so glad we had this opportunity to talk. I do hate to think I'm sneaking around behind Paula's back, but she worries enough as it is. I don't want to cause her any more anxiety. You won't say anything, will you? I mean about..." Doty started to calm down.

"Rest assured, Doty. I won't tell anyone what you told me and I certainly won't say a word to Paula. It's our secret." Realizing that she'd learned all this woman had to reveal for the moment, Eve thought it best to end the conversation before Paula returned. Until now, she'd been certain that Raul held the key to the mystery. Perhaps he still did, but in a different way. If only she knew where to find him. As much as she hated to admit it, Eve could understand how and why Raul was capable of killing Olive. These were new feelings for her and she didn't like them. She'd experienced too many new feelings lately that she didn't exactly care for. Her sense of justice had caused problems before, but never anything like this.

It took Eve a while to absorb everything she'd just heard. She wondered if her two neighbors were actually as innocent as they appeared. Didn't Doty's story contradict what she'd heard from Pearl Thomas? Was Doty lying? At first, Eve had thought Pearl might have been mistaken about what she'd heard, but now, she began to think it possible that Pearl might actually have lied. Rather than gaining a clearer picture of the events leading up to Olive's death, a seed of uncertainty began to take root in Eve's mind. Doty's story left her more confused than ever. She felt that she was going backwards rather than making any meaningful progress. Now, she had to face Adam. She knew exactly what he would say when she shared her latest discovery with him. Undoubtedly, he'd point out that there was still no hard evidence that a crime had been committed, only speculation. And, she conceded, on that point she was forced to agree.

"Thank you for coming, Eve. I feel so much better having talked to you about everything. It's easier when it's just the two of us, if you know what I mean."

"Of course. I hope I was helpful." Eve wondered if the woman would even mention their conversation to Paula. How suspicious she was becoming of everyone.

On her way home, Eve was deep in thought, reviewing all the bits and pieces of information she'd collected. The nagging feeling that someone, if not everyone, was hiding something was growing stronger. Could she be so wrong? For more than forty years, she had observed the behavior of children and teenagers. She knew when they were trying to cover up something they didn't want her to find out about. *Adults aren't that different,* she thought. Like children, they try to conceal their thoughts and actions, only they become more skillful about changing a sensitive subject or even avoiding it altogether. But, no matter what they said, or didn't say, Eve could generally sense when someone was being ingenuous. She had the same uneasy feelings now, but she didn't know what to do about them.

As she crossed the street, Eve's gaze was fixed on the ground and she didn't immediately notice the truck that came careening around the corner. She thought she heard a noise, turned her head and gave a start when, all of a sudden, she saw the dilapidated van bearing down on her. Before she had a chance to completely get out of the way, she fell to the ground and started rolling, barely avoiding being crushed by the heavy vehicle that just kept racing down the otherwise empty street.

Eve lay on the pavement, bruised and stunned. She assumed she must have screamed, because a few minutes later, several front doors opened and people came running out to see what had happened. The last thing she remembered before passing out was the sight of Adam rushing towards her.

Despite her fall, Eve was fortunate. No broken bones and no concussion. But, she'd have quite a few bruises and her body would ache for some time to come, the paramedics told Adam. It had only taken them about fifteen minutes to reach the scene after receiving a call from one of the local residents who heard the screaming. They wanted to take Eve to the hospital for further observation, but she refused. Finally, after much coaxing from Adam, she agreed to see a doctor the following day.

The paramedics stayed with Eve while Adam went home to get their car. When he returned, they helped him ease Eve into the back seat. The ambulance followed Adam and once he pulled into his driveway, the three men helped Eve into the house.

That evening, as she was lying in bed, Eve heard the murmur of voices coming from the living room. She tried to get up to find out what was happening, but quickly realized that moving around was going to be more difficult than anticipated. Reluctantly, she decided to wait for Adam to come to her. From the little she could hear, he was saying good night to someone whose voice she didn't recognize. *He'd be coming in to her in a few minutes,* she thought.

Eve pushed herself up in bed. She'd received more of a shock than anything else. Fortunately, she'd seen the truck at the last minute and managed to avoid being directly hit by it. With her eyes half closed, she listened to Adam, who was politely trying to end a conversation. She heard the front door close and, in another minute, her husband appeared in the bedroom doorway.

"Who was that?" Eve asked weakly, as she opened her eyes.

"The woman who lives on Calle del Sol. I don't know her name. She heard about the accident and wanted to see how you're doing. She said a lot of people are concerned about you. Apparently, you've become quite popular in this little town."

"Was it Mary?"

"I think that's her name. I've never really spoken to her before. She has a Southern accent. She seems very nice."

Eve opened her mouth to ask another question, but was interrupted by Adam before she could utter any words.

"How are you doing? Feeling any better?"

"Better than what? I haven't had time to feel better. All I know is that I ache all over."

"You're going to feel it for a while. That was a nasty fall you took. You're lucky you weren't hit by that truck." Adam tried to console his wife. "Let me get the heating pad. That should help a little." Adam walked over to the dresser and opened a drawer. He pulled out the pad, then plugged it into the wall outlet next to the bed, and helped Eve arrange it on her shoulder.

Eve moaned. She was not prepared to be laid up in bed and was determined that all she needed was a good night's sleep. "Did you see anything?" she asked her husband. It was still difficult for her to fully realize what had happened.

"I didn't really see much. I just heard a truck barreling down the street, then a scream, which, I presume, was you...and screeching brakes, but the driver just kept going."

"Did you see who was behind the wheel?" asked Eve.

"No, I'm sorry to say. I wish I had though. Whoever it was, he just kept going. I asked around and nobody seems to have seen either the truck or the driver."

"I wonder if..." Eve had difficulty finishing her sentence.

"What's that? What do you wonder?"

"No...it's too crazy..."

"Tell me what you're thinking," Adam encouraged.

"You don't think it could have been Raul who was driving the truck, do you?" Eve's voice began to tremble.

"That's enough," snapped Adam. "You've been so preoccupied with this whole mess, it nearly got you killed. I don't want to hear another word about Olive or Raul, or anyone else, for that matter. You need to focus on yourself. You're going to rest, whether you like it or not, and tomorrow, I'm taking you to see Doctor Valentine."

Eve raised her arm with difficulty and began to pat her stomach. "Okay...okay. I don't really want to see a doctor, but I'm much too weak to argue." Before closing her eyes, she smiled at Adam. He leaned over the bed and kissed her on the forehead.

"Good night, dear," he whispered softly. "See you in the morning. And try not to think too much, if that's at all possible."

Adam remained standing next to the bed and watched Eve until she fell asleep. As he looked down at her, a feeling of apprehension came over him. He realized how much he depended on this woman and he expected her to always be there for him. She gave him strength and brought meaning to his life. As far as he was concerned, they were inseparable and he couldn't bear the thought that something might happen to her now.

After a few minutes, Eve began to breathe deeply. *Finally,* thought Adam, *she will be able to get the sleep she desperately needs.* He hadn't mentioned it to her, but he'd been worried about the recent bouts of sleeplessness she'd been experiencing. He knew all too well that the circumstances surrounding Olive's death had been occupying her thoughts day and night.

Adam would sleep in the guest room, but later. Right now, he wanted to stay with his wife for a while.

On the surface, everyday life in Sunshine Valley contrasted dramatically with the area's turbulent past. The desert that surrounded the peaceful community had once been the home of the Apache Indians. Rich deposits of silver had lured miners to the neighboring hills and many had to pay for their newly discovered treasures with their blood. In the middle of the nineteenth century, the main road that led into the valley had been a wagon route connecting Tucson and Nogales. At first, it had been the scene of bloody battles between Mexicans and Apaches. Later, the victims were American miners and ranchers. Gradually, the area stabilized, tamed, in part, by the onslaught of land developers and "snowbirds" who came from all parts of the country to find their "El Dorado."

Sunset was perhaps the most picturesque time of day in Sunshine Valley and today was no exception. An endless variety of cloud formations moved slowly across the red sky, casting shadows on the washes and gullies and cutting across the ridges and peaks of the Santa Catalina mountains. Margarita Creek, normally dry, flowed and bubbled across the landscape of high desert scrub. Only a relatively new sign by the side of the road provided a hint that the valley might not have completely escaped its violent past. It warned against the use of firearms, noting that the area was frequented by birdwatchers and hikers.

Two such admirers of the desert landscape, a man and a woman out for a late afternoon hike, were making their way back across the sand back to the main road when they noticed the large birds flying in a circle overhead.

"Looks like vultures," said the woman as she pointed to the sky.

"Awful things. There's probably some garbage or a dead animal nearby," replied her companion.

The last rays of sunlight lingered on the upper edges of the clouds. The end of yet another perfect day, the couple assured one another. They kept walking and laughed and talked about what they should have for dinner that evening.

As they made their way along a narrow path, the woman squinted, trying to identify a dark silhouette that was lying on the ground a few yards in front of them. *A boulder,* she thought. But, as the two hikers approached the hazy form, they both stopped suddenly and turned to each other in horror. Directly in front of them, sprawled out on the ground, in the middle of the path, lay the carcass of a man whose feet were tangled in a growth of scrub. His clothes were torn, and large parts of his flesh appeared to have been eaten away by coyotes and vultures.

The couple stopped suddenly, as if paralyzed. They seemed unable to fully comprehend what they were witnessing. The woman gasped, stumbled backwards, and barely avoided falling over a cactus. Her companion grabbed her arms and pulled her to his chest.

"What should we do?" she asked, choking on her words.

"We have to call the police," he said, shaken. "Come on...quickly...let's get out of here and find a phone." The man grabbed the woman's hand and they both began running away from the terrifying scene.

About thirty minutes later, a series of flashing red lights appeared along the main road, sirens wailing. It was an odd sight to see in the middle of the serene desert. Several people had come out of nearby houses when they heard all the activity and a crowd began to gather along the road, near where the body was found. An ambulance pulled up and two men climbed out. They lifted a stretcher from the rear of the vehicle, spoke to the two hikers, then marched into the desert. After a few minutes, they returned, carrying what appeared to be a body that was covered with a sheet.

"Did you see who it was?" the onlookers asked each other.

"Hard to tell...looks like a man, though."

"Probably been there for awhile."

People came and went all evening, uncertain what they would find. No one knew for sure who the dead man was, but everybody had an opinion about how he died.

'Heart attack," said one.

"Could be suicide...did they find a gun?"

"Possibly an accident," volunteered another." Maybe he tripped and fell. It's easy to catch your foot on this scrub and lose your balance. I've done it many times."

The speculation continued. It had been a busy evening for the local residents. Finally, around nine o'clock, the crowd began to thin out and the last of the curiosity-seekers returned to the safety of their homes. Despite the outward calm, many of the lights in the red-tiled stucco houses of Sunshine Valley burned later than usual that night. It had also been a busy evening for the paramedics. In fact, it was the first time that they'd received two urgent calls within such a short time.

Chapter 11

After sitting by his wife for almost an hour, Adam stood up and went into the guest bedroom, where he quickly got into bed. Overcome by the scare of Eve's accident, he immediately fell into a deep sleep. At some point during the night, he began to dream. The boys were playing baseball in the street. One of the girls who was watching climbed into a tree to get a better look. She slipped, fell to the ground and lay there, motionless. One of the boys saw his sister fall and tried to call out to her, but she didn't respond. She couldn't hear him because he was unable to make a sound, even though he was trying to shout as loud as he could. Why wouldn't his mouth cooperate? He tried to formulate words, but could only make incomprehensible gurgling noises as he rolled back and forth.

After endless tossing and turning in the strange bed, Adam finally opened his eyes and looked around the room, momentarily disoriented and agitated. Nothing looked familiar. Where was he? Seldom had he spent such a restless night in which sleep, rather than providing comfort, filled his mind with images of long-forgotten horror. His mouth was dry and he had difficulty swallowing. He looked down and saw that he had kicked off the blanket and sheet that covered him and apparently, he'd begun ripping away at the bottom fitted sheet as well. He took a deep breath and exhaled slowly, glad to finally be awake. A dim ray of light broke through the window and Adam finally began to recognize some familiar objects.

The moaning and groaning that had seemed part of an endless nightmare grew louder. But, these sounds of distress were not a dream. They were coming from the other bedroom. Suddenly, the events of the preceding evening came rushing into Adam's consciousness and he called out to Eve. She responded with another moan as he jumped out of bed and ran to her. He had no idea of the time. The gray light coming through the window provided no clue. It was either very early or late and overcast.

In his haste, Adam tripped over the rug that ran the length of the hallway. As he stumbled into the master bedroom head first, swearing under his breath, he looked up at Eve who was lying in bed motionless, eyes wide open. Coco was lying next to her and jumped down when he saw Adam.

"You better be careful or we'll both be laid up," she said, chuckling at the sight of her disheveled husband.

Still not fully awake, Adam gazed stupidly at his wife for a few seconds. Coco began running around and started barking. She wasn't used to all the unfamiliar noises that filled the room. "It's only me, Coco," he said, bending down to scratch the dog's ear.

"You look like you've had a pretty wild night," Eve continued, still smiling.

Adam pushed back his hair and rolled down a pajama leg that had inched its way up his right calf. "Just a little skydiving," he replied. "But, I must say, you look pretty good this morning, at least for someone who nearly got herself run over."

"Looks can be deceiving," she flinched, trying to raise herself up. "What hit me, anyway?"

"I'm afraid you're going to feel it today." Adam walked over to the bed and put his hand on her forehead.

"I don't have a temperature," she said petulantly.

"I know...but there's no harm in checking."

"Every bone in my body aches," she exclaimed, full of reawakened pain.

"Well, I'm not surprised. You had a very nasty fall."

"Suddenly, I'm aware of parts of my body I didn't even know existed."

"Try not to move around so much."

Eve raised her eyebrows and Adam kissed her on the cheek. "Does it look like I'm going anywhere?" She started to laugh. "I haven't been this sore since I first took up golf."

Adam was relieved to find his wife in such good spirits, despite her discomfort. *How fortunate she'd been,* he thought. Judging by the skid marks on the pavement, she'd escaped being run over by less than a foot.

"You know, that was such a close call. You're lucky you didn't break anything."

"Please," groaned Eve. "That's all I need."

"Well, I'm taking you to see Dr. Valentine today. I want to make sure everything's in place."

"No," she protested weakly. "I'll be okay. All I need is a little rest. I don't want to go to the doctor."

"Yes, I know you're going to be all right, but, to be on the safe side, I think we ought to let Dr. Valentine have a look. I trust him. If there's anything that's the least bit out of kilter, he'll find it and fix it. We're very lucky he's here in Tucson."

Eve had managed to push herself up into a sitting position. Exasperated, she shrugged her shoulders and sighed.

"Now I know what you must have looked like when you were a little girl," Adam teased.

"Hmmm...well, this little girl is starving," she complained.

"I'm going to make breakfast right now...eggs okay?"

Eve nodded and closed her eyes.

After several minutes, Adam reentered the bedroom, carrying a tray filled with a wide assortment of food. He'd made scrambled eggs, bacon, a stack of toast, orange juice, and coffee.

"My goodness...looks like we're having a party," Eve exclaimed, surprised at the amount of food her husband had prepared. "Is someone joining us?"

"Well, you said you were starving. Just eat what you want."

"I need a fork," she said enthusiastically, eyeing the colorful display that Adam had placed across her lap.

By the time he returned from the kitchen, Eve was on her second piece of toast.

"You know," she said with an air of contentment, "I believe this is the best toast I've ever eaten."

"I'll give you the recipe," replied her husband.

Eve continued chewing as Adam left the room to phone the doctor. She admired his efficiency, but how she hated this feeling of helplessness!

"We're in luck. Dr. Valentine will see us as soon as we can make it into Tucson. When I told him what happened to you, he said to come right over."

"I really don't think it's necessary," Eve pleaded in vain. "Why do we have to go all the way to Tucson, anyway? There are plenty of doctors here in Sunshine Valley."

"Yes, of course, there are doctors here, but I know Martin. He's a friend. We used to work together at the hospital in San Diego and I trust his judgment. He has a very busy practice, but said he'd squeeze you in...anything for an Iverson...no problem. Now, let me help you get out of bed." Eve had barely finished eating as Adam moved the tray off the bed and on to the night stand.

"I think I can manage alone," she said, lifting herself up slowly.

"Are you sure?"

"Yes. You go and get yourself dressed." Determined, Eve raised herself up and out of bed. Adam stood by, watching, and waiting to help. "Go on...go on," she insisted. I'm perfectly capable of getting dressed by myself."

"You really are stubborn," sighed Adam as Eve shooed him out of the room.

She slowly made her way to the closet and looked for something suitable, but simple to wear, finally settling on an oversized flowered dress that she could slip into and out of with little difficulty. Ten minutes later, she was sitting on the edge of the bed, waiting patiently for her husband to return. When he appeared, she couldn't help but smile. Adam was wearing a tight fitting Western-style shirt and bolo tie, beaming from ear to ear. If he felt self-conscious, he tried not to show it. He held out his arm and slowly led Eve to the front door.

"You watch things here, Coco," he turned and said to the poodle whose tail was wagging, hoping that she would be going with them. "We won't be long."

Adam slowly escorted Eve out of the house and over to the car. He opened the front door on the passenger's side. "It might be easier for you in the back seat, but I want you next to me," he said as he eased her into the seat. "If you're too uncomfortable, just let me know and I'll help you get in back."

Eve agreed and slowly eased her way into the passenger seat. As they began driving, she turned to Adam and spoke. "You know, from the little I saw, it seemed like that truck was aiming right for me. Maybe

I'm imagining it, but, the driver couldn't have come any closer if he tried."

"You were very lucky he didn't hit you," said Adam.

"Well, one good thing...at least I know my reflexes are still working. I happened to look up at the right moment and noticed the truck. A second or two more and it would have been too late."

"You didn't hear anything?" Adam asked.

"I thought I heard something, but wasn't sure what it was. I was deep in thought and everything happened so quickly. Fortunately, I looked up, but there wasn't time to do anything except get out of the way as fast as possible. I must have tripped. I always did have weak ankles, you know."

"Yes, I remember. We never fared well at winter sports."

Eve laughed, remembering the many futile attempts she'd made to go ice skating when she was younger. Somehow, she'd always manage to twist her ankle and fall, pulling Adam down on top of her.

"I spent more time on my bottom than I did on my feet, didn't I?"

"You mean, we did, don't you? You always seemed to take me with you, as I recall," replied Adam.

"It's a good thing we don't have much ice here," said Eve, as they both laughed.

Eve surveyed the quiet street. Except for a man and a woman who were out jogging, it was empty. "I don't suppose anyone else saw the driver?" she asked after a while.

"No, I don't think so. At least, nobody has reported anything. Actually, we were kind of hoping you might have seen something."

"We?" Eve was surprised by her husband's remark. It hadn't occurred to her that he might have discussed the accident with anyone.

"Sheriff Warner stopped by late last night to ask you some questions, but you'd already gone to sleep and I thought it best not to disturb you. He said he'd come back again later today to talk with you." Adam had avoided mentioning the visit earlier since he didn't want to upset Eve any more than necessary. The deputy had arrived at the house as Adam was getting ready for bed. He apologized for the late visit, then went on to explain about the discovery of the dead body on the prairie.

"I don't have anything to say to him. What does he want to talk to me about, anyway?" Eve asked, apprehensively.

"He just wants to ask you a few questions. He thought you might be able to shed some light on the driver of the truck. The person should be found."

"And given a ticket...because that's just about all this deputy is capable of doing. I wouldn't expect too much from him if I were you."

"I don't, but he still wants to ask you a few questions."

Eve winced as Adam hit a pot hole.

"Sorry," he apologized and rolled down the window.

"That's what we need," said Eve, wiping her forehead. "It's warmer today than I thought it would be."

They both settled back to enjoy the view. The desert was in full bloom.

"So, you didn't recognize the driver?" Adam asked after a while.

"You may think this is strange, but, actually, I thought I did."

"Really? Who did you see?" Adam looked away from the road for a second, then swerved to avoid a ball of tumbleweed that was headed towards the car.

"I can't be completely certain, but I thought the driver looked very much like Raul," continued Eve.

"Raul?...Why on earth would he want to hit you?"

"I have no idea. I've been wondering the same thing myself. Who knows? I was wrong before when I thought I saw him raking leaves. Maybe my mind was playing tricks on me. It wouldn't be the first time."

"What do you remember seeing?" Adam urged her to continue.

"It was one of those beat up old used-to-be-white trucks that the gardeners drive. Raul has one exactly like it, or, at least he shares it with someone. I didn't notice anything special about it...just the same as all the others. That's about it. That's all I can tell you. I'm not sure who was driving, but I'm positive about the truck."

"Did you happen to get a license number?" Adam asked, knowing the answer in advance.

Eve shook her head. "Everything happened too fast."

"Yes and the truck was going fast...thank goodness it didn't hit you."

"Speaking of fast," said Eve as she pointed to the speedometer, "are you trying to keep up with your age? What's the big hurry?"

"I thought you were anxious to get this over with..."

"Don't worry, I'm fine with it all...but, I think it's better if we get to Tucson and back home in one piece." Eve turned to her husband and smiled.

Adam eased his foot off the accelerator as he continued driving down the highway. After another fifteen minutes, he turned into the complex that housed several doctors' offices. He drove around several times until he noticed someone who was just pulling out of a space in front of a small building, then parked the car. "Sit here until I come back for you," he said to Eve. "I want to find the office first and not have you walk more than necessary.

Once Adam located the sign that read Martin Valentine, M.D., he returned to the car and led Eve up the ramp. As the couple entered the crowded waiting room, a row of heads turned to look at them. Men and women of all sizes and ages sat in uncomfortable looking chairs, waiting to be called into another room, some more restless than others. Eve sniffed and wrinkled her nose. She hated the smell of anything medicinal. She was about to turn and make an exit, when she felt Adam take her by the arm and lead her to the one empty chair at the far side of the room.

"Please try to relax. You're not going anywhere and you're not making this any easier," he admonished.

"Well, really, if there were something wrong with me, but I'm fine, just a few aches and pains. I shouldn't be taking up the doctor's time. He has all these other people to take care of," she said, waving her right arm across the room.

"Sit," commanded Adam.

Eve frowned, but obeyed. "You sound like you're talking to Coco."

"She's much easier to handle than you are."

As Eve sat down, Adam walked over to the receptionist and gave their name. "Oh, yes," said the woman, as she smiled politely. "We're expecting you. Please sit down. I'll tell Dr. Valentine you're here. He's with a patient right now, but it won't be long. He'll see you as soon as he's finished."

Adam thanked the woman, then completed a short questionnaire. When he finished, he turned around to survey the waiting room. Since there was no place for him to sit, he receded into a corner and leaned against the wall until a chair was vacated. He didn't have to wait long. As he stood leafing through an old fishing magazine, the door to the inner office opened and a nurse appeared. She smiled and asked Eve to follow her. All eyes glared at her as she slowly pushed herself out of the chair. She had suddenly become very unpopular with the other patients. Why didn't she have to wait her turn like everyone else? One woman who had obviously been waiting a long time became quite vocal and asked the receptionist why certain people seemed to get special privileges. As soon as the door closed behind Eve, the woman turned her gaze towards Adam, who simply shrugged his shoulders and sat down in the empty chair.

Each person in the waiting room appeared to have a different way of passing the time. Some of the patients read magazines and newspapers. Others did crossword puzzles. Still others were busy on their cell phones. Adam became particularly fascinated by an elderly woman who sat opposite him doing needlepoint. Although gnarled and misshapen, her fingers moved swiftly and skillfully, filling in a large yellow shape. He picked up another magazine and looked around at the other people who were waiting. Almost apologetically, he smiled at two sets of eyes that were staring at him from across the room. Finally, they looked away.

Settling back in his chair, Adam made a mental calculation of all the years he'd spent in an office not too different from this one. He recognized the smell and, unlike Eve, it made him nostalgic. He had started out to be a doctor himself, but his career, like so many others, had been cut short by the Vietnam war. When, after four years of active duty, he returned home to California, and with a young wife, a Navy lieutenant named Eve Lind whom he'd met in Washington, he felt too much time had elapsed for him to go back to medicine, so he settled on hospital administration instead. Although it wasn't his first choice, he never regretted the decision. It was a career that, through the years, had brought him great satisfaction. It was odd, he reflected, how all these offices resemble each other. The familiarity brought him a much needed sense of comfort.

After what seemed like a reasonable amount of time, Adam looked at his watch. He wondered how long the exam was going to take. Surely, Eve would be emerging from the inner office any minute. None of the magazines interested him. Several people had dozed off and were snoring. The woman with the needlepoint was working just as quickly as before. Adam stood up and stretched his arms. Apparently, this was an unusual activity, because, once again, several eyes focused on him. Who does he think he is? They seemed to be questioning.

Once again, Adam sat down, resigned, like the others, to the seemingly interminable wait. He thought about Eve and that quality of dogged persistence that had brought her here. If it hadn't been for the investigation she'd taken upon herself to conduct, she wouldn't have had the accident. But, he knew it was useless to pursue that line of reasoning. Eve had an unwavering sense of justice and no amount of arguing could shake her beliefs. When she put her mind to something, there was no stopping her.

It was this same determination that had landed Eve in trouble before. Adam smiled, recalling how, years earlier, on a trip to New York, she'd pursued a mugger she spotted in Central Park. She and Adam had been strolling through the park one sunny afternoon, when, amid the steady stream of pedestrians, joggers, and bicyclists, she noticed a man hitting a woman over the head with a purse that he'd just grabbed from her. Without saying a word, Eve ran after the thief, then began shouting at him to drop the purse. Suddenly, everyone in the area stopped what they were doing and several young men joined her in pursuit of the culprit.

Eventually, they caught him, knocked him to the ground, called the police, and were able to return the purse to the woman. In spite of her heroic act, however, the police warned her about such practice in the future. No, if somebody was guilty of wrongdoing, it would be best not to cross the path of Eve Iverson.

Adam must have dozed off at some point. The room was hot and stuffy and since he'd experienced a restless night, it was difficult for him to keep his eyes open. After an indeterminate amount of time, he was awakened by the sound of someone calling his name.

"Adam," said Eve softly, shaking his shoulder.

He opened his eyes and looked sheepishly around the room. It was the first time he could remember falling asleep in public. "Well, what's the verdict?" He stood up, yawned, then returned Eve's broad smile.

"I wasn't sure what would happen, but I must say it was much easier than I thought it would be. I like him...Dr. Valentine." Eve was obviously relieved. It had never occurred to Adam that she might be afraid. But, all he had to do was take one look at his wife to realize that a heavy burden had been lifted. She looked radiant. The glow in her cheeks and the way she threw her head back as she laughed made her appear much younger than her actual age.

"What did he say? Is everything okay?" Adam asked.

"Nothing broken. No concussion. Other than being about ten pounds overweight, which, by the way, I didn't need him to tell me, I'm fine...only a few bruises. He did a few tests and said he'd call us with the results as soon as he got them, but he didn't seem too concerned. He just told me to get a lot of rest and let you take good care of me. He was very nice. He gave me a prescription for pain killers, if things got too bad, but I think I'm going to start out with a heating pad. At the risk of sounding like Olive, I have to say I don't like to take drugs."

Adam had the impression that Eve wanted to put her arms around him, but, because of all the eyes that were focused on them, she held back.

"I'm afraid, however, that I won't be able to go dancing for a while," she teased.

"Or play golf," he added.

"I'm not sure that matters too much, considering the way I play."

"At least now you have a good excuse." Adam looked at her expectantly, not really certain what to do next. He was waiting for a cue from her and it wasn't long in coming.

"Let's get out of here...I want to go home now," she said with a burst of enthusiasm.

Was that a wink she gave him as she turned to open the door? He got up from his chair and followed her.

"That really looks nice," said Adam as he passed the woman who was doing the needlepoint. She looked up and, for a moment, seemed surprised that someone was speaking to her. Smiling broadly, she thanked Adam for the compliment.

"What's that? What looks nice?" Eve asked, turning around.

"You dear...you look nice," replied Adam.

Eve raised her eyebrows. *Had she missed something?* she wondered. "What are you talking about?" she asked quizzically.

"Nothing. I was just talking to someone else, that's all."

When they reached the car, Eve stopped for a moment and stared straight ahead with a puzzled look on her face.

"What's the matter?" Adam asked, concerned.

"I'm thinking," she replied.

"How about thinking in the car?" said Adam as he opened the door.

She didn't respond, but slowly lowered herself into the front seat. Adam had difficulty suppressing a smile. Eve's brain cells were at work again and he knew it was useless to interrupt her or try to dissuade her from her thoughts.

"Adam," she began, after a few minutes, "you were speaking to that woman."

"Which woman?" He had no idea where this line of questioning was going, but was certain it had a purpose.

"The woman who was doing the needlepoint...you were talking to her when we were leaving the doctor's office," said Eve. "You weren't talking to me."

"Yes, I'm sorry if it made you jealous," he said jokingly.

"Humor me, Adam, but, don't patronize me."

"Sorry, dear, but, I have absolutely no idea what you're talking about or where you're going with this."

"What was it you said?" continued Eve.

"What did I say? What do you mean?"

"Yes...when we were leaving the doctor's office...what was it you said?"

"I don't know. I guess I said 'that's very nice,' or something to that effect."

"No. What was it you said to me?" Eve persisted,

"I said I was talking to someone else. You thought I was talking to you, I guess."

Eve burst into laughter. "You, my gifted husband, are a genius," she exclaimed. "Did I ever tell you that?"

Adam was still having difficulty following his wife's line of thinking. Was he being obtuse, or was there some logic to her questions? He was at a total loss for an answer. "Thank you, dear, but, can you tell me what brilliant thing I've done this time?"

Eve was about to explain, but thought better of it. She felt that more urgent matters needed to be addressed first. "Let's go home," she repeated. "I'll explain everything to you later."

The ride back to Sunshine Valley was a quiet one. Eve looked out the window, admiring what she saw. "It's really lovely here now," she said," but I wonder how we will be able to endure the summers. It got a bit toasty last July and August."

"We can always drive up to the mountains when it gets too hot...Prescott...or Sedona. From what I gather, many of the people who live here year 'round rent a cottage for a few weeks someplace where it's cooler. That could be kind of fun. We can't do it this summer because of our trip, but perhaps next year. We might even want to do a little hiking...you should be all healed by then."

Eve simply nodded. She didn't say another word during the remainder of the trip back home. As they turned off the main highway, she finally broke the silence. "Thank you, Adam, for taking me to see Dr. Valentine. I'm really glad we went there...you have no idea how glad."

Adam was pleased as well, but, he was certain it was for a different reason. "Are you ever going to tell me what's on your mind?" he asked. I know you're thinking about something and I'm quite sure it doesn't have to do with your fall." It was obvious that his wife had been deep in thought during the entire trip back to Sunshine Valley, but it wasn't like her not to tell her husband if something was bothering her.

"Tell you?" she asked.

"What's on your mind? I could hear your brain churning away all the way back."

"Yes, of course, I'll tell you."

Knowing he would have to wait until Eve was ready to share her thoughts, Adam made an attempt to lighten the conversation. "This is like one of your Sunday crosswords, isn't it? You're just as obsessed."

"Yes," she agreed, smiling. "I do seem to like following clues to find answers. But, it's more like a Saturday puzzle. Sunday's may take longer to solve, but eventually I get the answers. Saturday's is impossible."

As they pulled into the driveway, Eve took a deep breath and said, "This is nice. I'm so glad to be back home." When Adam opened the front door, Coco came running, tale wagging high in the air. He'd closed the windows and drapes before leaving, so the house was about ten degrees cooler than the air outside. Although everything seemed so normal, both Adam and Eve knew things were far from normal.

"I'm doing the cooking tonight," Adam declared, once they were inside, "doctor's orders." He prided himself on his culinary expertise. At least once a week, he would prepare a gourmet dinner for the two of them. Eve would have liked for him to cook more often, but since she was left with the clean up, once a week was more than enough for her. Although the end result was always spectacular, when Adam finished, it usually looked as if a cyclone had passed through the kitchen. She wondered how he could use so many pots and pans and why he needed so many different utensils.

"Does that mean I have to clean up?" she asked hesitantly, hoping Adam would pick up on her reticence. .

"No, dear...I'll do both this time. You're just going to relax and force yourself to be waited on. Now, tell me, what would you like?"

"I really don't care that much...something simple."

"Boeuf Bourginon? Coq au Vin? You name it. Anything your heart desires."

"Eggs," Eve stated emphatically.

"What?"

"Oeufs," she repeated, in French, "scrambled oeufs."

"Are you sure? You had eggs for breakfast."

"I know and they were delicious. That's why I'd like the same thing. Besides, you don't need a lot of pots and pans to make eggs."

"But, I'd like to make you something special."

"Next week...you can make something fancy next week when I'm feeling better. I'll appreciate it more. Right now, eggs are fine."

Adam was disappointed, but chose not to try and dissuade his wife.

In all the confusion, Eve had not found an opportunity tell her husband about the conversation she'd had with Doty. She asked him to sit down with her on the living room couch and explained that she had something important to tell him.

"I hope it doesn't have to do with Olive," said Adam cautiously. "I was rather hoping that we were headed in a new direction and that you would put all of the turmoil out of your mind after what happened."

"You're not serious, I hope. There's still a killer on the loose, you know. How can I put that out of my mind?"

"I know there's a killer loose. That's what I'm afraid of. What makes you think you aren't his next target?" Adam spoke slowly, assuming his most serious tone.

"What do you mean?" asked Eve.

"I'm serious and I'm very concerned about you. With all the questions you've been asking, what makes you think that the person driving the truck didn't intend to run you over on purpose?"

"Don't be ridiculous. I really don't think anyone has it in for me." Eve dismissed her husband's warnings and continued recounting the details of her meeting with Doty.

"At first, I was confused when Doty told me she heard Olive yelling at Raul for being lazy, and, yet, Pearl had said she heard Olive calling someone a criminal. I thought perhaps one of them was mistaken. I even considered the possibility that one of them might be lying, but I couldn't figure out a reason for not telling the truth."

Eve watched Adam carefully as she spoke, checking his reaction to her every word. Realizing that it would be futile to try and stop her, he made no attempt to discourage or interrupt her and continued quietly listening to her account. Since he hadn't heard anything firsthand, he could only base any opinion he might formulate on what his wife was telling him, so he paid close attention to what she had to say.

After a few moments, Adam began to express what he thought was a reasonable explanation. "If Pearl said she heard one thing and Doty another, maybe one of them was mistaken, or maybe they each heard a different part of the conversation, or..."

"Or, maybe," Eve interrupted, "Olive was yelling at two different people at two different times. That's the connection I was looking for. Now, it makes sense." She leaned back and smiled broadly. "See what I meant when I called you a genius?"

"So, that's what all that business at the doctor's office was about?"

"Exactly. Since you were right behind me as we were leaving Dr. Valentine's office, I thought you were talking to me, but you weren't. I couldn't see you because my back was turned. You were talking to someone else. See what I mean? I always assumed Olive was just yelling at one person. She could very easily have been yelling at two different people, at two different times."

"Yes...You make a good point. Doty heard Olive yelling at..."

Eve completed his sentence. "Raul."

"And Pearl and Tom heard her yelling at..."

"Someone else...the killer, perhaps?" said Eve.

It took Adam a moment to absorb everything he'd just heard, then stared at Eve, face frozen, as he suddenly realized the meaning of her words. "I think you better be careful about doing any more investigating on your own. It's getting too dangerous. Let's talk to the deputy when he comes here. You can tell him what you just told me."

Eve raised her arm and cringed in pain. She'd momentarily forgotten about her condition and wanted to slap the arm of her chair in protest to Adam's suggestion, but was unable to get any leverage.

"Absolutely not," she said, gritting her teeth. "Promise me you won't say anything to him." She began to rub her arm and looked at Adam.

"Only if you promise to take it easy. You said that Dr. Valentine told you to rest."

"I'm fine," she protested.

"Promise me you won't go doing any more investigating on your own. I don't think you realize how dangerous it is to go poking into other people's lives, especially when one of them might be a killer. Don't forget the trouble you almost got into in New York..."

"All right, I promise...but, please don't say anything to that deputy, at least, not yet," Eve begged.

Their conversation was interrupted by the ringing of the doorbell.

"There he is now," said Adam, as he got up and went to open the front door.

"I caught you this time. I came by earlier, but you were out." A tall, uniformed man stood squarely in the doorway.

"We were in Tucson...I brought Eve to see a doctor," explained Adam.

"That's what I figured."

Adam led the deputy into the living room and Eve managed to produce a thin smile.

"Lots of excitement around here," said the deputy.

The man with the holster slung low around his waist took off his hat and walked over to Eve. She noticed the pearl handle revolver and the silver cartridges and wondered if it wasn't mostly for show.

"Oh, it wasn't anything much," said Eve, self-consciously, thinking he was referring to her accident.

"No? It's not every day we find a dead body," replied the deputy.

Eve frowned. She looked at the man in disbelief. *Was he insensitive as well as incompetent?* she wondered. "Well, I wouldn't exactly say I'm ready to be buried yet," she said, curtly.

"Not you, Mrs. Iverson." He laughed and scratched his head. "You probably haven't heard, but someone found the body of a dead man out on the prairie last night."

Eve was stunned by the news and turned to Adam. "Did you hear that?"

"Yes. Bud told me last night," replied Adam.

"And you didn't tell me?" She looked at her husband in disbelief.

"Well..." began Adam, searching in vain for an explanation.

"Who was it?" Eve asked, ignoring her husband.

"Mexican fellow...used to be a gardener here."

"Oh, my God," gasped Eve, "Raul."

"That's right, ma'am...Raul Valdez. But, how'd you know? We only identified the body this morning."

"I didn't know. But, I know he's been missing for a week."

"Probably been dead that long from what I could tell."

Eve looked at Adam. She felt sickened by the news, but wanted to know more. Adam's face had lost all color as the deputy began to recount the details surrounding the discovery of Raul's body.

"I figure he got drunk, wandered off the road, tripped and hit his head. We found an empty bottle of tequila next to him. You know how it is with these fellows."

"No," said Eve curtly, "how is it?"

Eve felt her anger rising. She detested the presumptions people made about the gardeners in Sunshine Valley.

Adam glanced at his wife and signaled her to keep still. Then, he turned to the deputy. "I'm sorry, Bud, but Eve's not feeling too well," he explained.

"I understand. I'll try not to bother you too much. I only have a few questions."

Eve was unable to provide any meaningful information about the driver of the truck that hit her. She answered the deputy's questions as directly and briefly as possible, anxious for him to leave.

"Well, thank you. I'll let you know if we come up with anything." Putting his note pad in his shirt pocket, Deputy Warner prepared to leave.

"What are you going to do about Raul?" Eve asked.

"What do you mean? Not much we can do. No family that we know of."

Adam thanked the officer for coming before Eve had a chance to say anything further and offered to see him to his car. When he returned, he went directly to the table where he kept his pipes. He picked one up and lit it, then walked over to the window and looked out. After a few moments, Eve broke the silence.

"Isn't it terrible?" he said.

"Yes...it is. Poor Raul...I knew something was wrong It wasn't like him to just disappear without saying anything."

"And he didn't drink," added Adam.

"How do you know that?"

"I offered him a beer a couple of months ago when he was digging up a cactus out front. He looked hot and I thought he might be thirsty. He thanked me, but refused. He said he couldn't drink alcohol."

"Why not?"

"He had ulcers."

"Oh, Adam," Eve gasped.

There it was. The nightmare continued. Someone else in Sunshine Valley had been murdered.

Chapter 12

"Sunshine Valley Realty. How can I help you?" The voice on the other end of the phone sounded young and cheerful.

"This is Adam Iverson. I'm trying to locate some people and I wonder if you might be able help me."

"Yes? I'll see what I can do. Why don't you tell me who it is you're looking for."

"About a week ago, one of your realtors, Dave Wilcox, showed a house on Camino Avion to a couple...from Illinois, I think. It's very important that I get in touch with them and I was wondering if you happen to know their name or where they might be staying."

"I'm really sorry, I'd love to help you, but we're not allowed to give out such information," replied the voice.

Adam could picture the woman at the other end of the line, efficient and protective. She politely explained how it was against company policy to disclose any information about current or potential clients.

"I understand, but this is urgent. I need to locate them," Adam insisted.

"I'm so sorry...I really can't help you. Is there anything else I might be able to assist you with?" She wasn't going to budge.

Adam was beginning to lose his patience and decided to try a different tactic. "Let me assure you, it has nothing to do with real estate," he started to explain.

"It's about stamps. The man is a stamp collector and so am I. I just want to talk to him about his collection."

Adam wondered if the woman would believe his story. He was well aware that stamp collectors were known for their occasional fanatical behavior, so he thought it didn't seem too farfetched that he might be trying to locate another collector. But, he concluded, this woman probably didn't understand the obsession, or perhaps she just didn't care.

"Would you mind if I get back to you?" she asked. "I'm all alone here and have to wait and ask my boss if it's okay to give out that information. I'll find out what I can, then call you."

"Why don't you also ask Dave when he comes in if he could give me a call," said Adam. He thanked the woman, then hung up, sat back, and waited.

After about thirty minutes, the phone began to ring. Adam picked up the receiver and heard the same young woman's voice. "This is Ellen from Sunshine Realty, returning your call," she announced in a friendly, but restrained voice. "I'm afraid Dave Wilcox isn't here now, but I left a message for him. He'll probably call you later. I asked a few people in the office, but nobody seems to know the couple you're referring to...so, I can't tell you their name or where they're staying," she said apologetically.

"Are you certain?" Adam persisted.

"Yes, I'm afraid I can't help you. They may even have returned to Illinois by now, if that's where you say they're from."

"Yes, I think that's what they said."

"Are you sure you have the right realty company? There are several others here in Sunshine..."

Adam didn't wait for her to finish. "Yes, I'm positive. As I told you, they were with Dave Wilcox."

"Well, I'm sorry, I can't help you," the woman repeated. Was there something unnatural about her voice? A hint, perhaps, that indicated she'd been told not to divulge any information? Realizing that he'd get no further, Adam thanked her, hung up, and tried another number.

After three rings, a man's voice answered.

"Hello, Bill? This is Adam Iverson. I have a question and I think you're the only one who might be able to help me. Do you happen to know the name of the people Dave Wilcox showed your house to the morning Olive Howell died?" Adam didn't waste any time and came straight to the point. He was eager to get in touch with the couple as quickly as possible, that is, if they were still in town.

"You mean the Wentworths?"

"Are they the ones?"

"Yes, that's their name," Bill replied. "Anyway, that's what Dave Wilcox told me."

"Do you know where they're staying?"

"The Villas...why?"

Adam ignored the question. "Do you think they're still in town?" he asked, anxiously.

"I'm pretty sure. I ran into them the other day. They're still here and, from what I understand, still looking...but why do you want to know where they're staying?" Bill asked again.

There was a long pause. "Thanks for your help," responded Adam, ignoring the question.

Bill was concerned about the tone in Adam's voice. "Is something wrong?" he asked.

"No, everything's fine. I just want to get in touch with them before they leave...it's about some stamps, that's all."

"Stamps?" The man sounded puzzled.

Adam didn't want to make up another lie, so he quickly thanked Bill, then hung up. He called the Operator to get the correct phone number and was quickly connected. "Valley Villas," answered an elderly sounding female voice, "how may I help you?"

"I wonder if you happen to have a Mr. and Mrs. Wentworth staying at the Villas?" Adam asked politely.

"Yes, they're here," responded the woman.

"Good. Could you tell me what number they're in?"

"I'm sorry...I can't..."

Adam didn't let her finish. "I have a book of theirs that I borrowed and I want to return it before they go back home to Illinois."

"Well, I'm not sure..."

Adam assumed his most professional and reassuring tone. "It's perfectly all right. I know they're going back to Illinois soon and I'd like to drop the book off this afternoon before they leave." His voice left no room for doubt.

"Number 63 Paseo Quinto," responded the woman, somewhat reluctantly. "But, you can leave the book with me, here at the office, if you like...I'd be more than happy to give it to them and save you the trouble..."

Adam could hardly believe his good fortune. He didn't let the woman finish. He simply thanked her, then hung up. Rising to his feet, he looked at his watch. It was already past eleven o'clock. He went into the bedroom to speak to Eve who was resting on the bed.

"Will you be okay if I go out for a while?" he asked.

She wasn't sleeping, but her eyes were closed, her German book lying open next to her. "Where are you going?" she managed to mumble.

"I have to see somebody about some stamps."

"Stamps?" she asked vaguely.

Obsessions can sometimes come in very handy, thought Adam. He could always use his stamp collection as an excuse for any erratic behavior that he might exhibit.

Once again, the phone started ringing and Adam left the room to answer it. When he returned a few minutes later, he was smiling broadly. "That was Dr. Valentine. He was calling with your test results and to see how you're doing. He was very pleased and said everything looks good. What you need most is rest. I'm a little hesitant to tell you this, but he even thought some time in the Jacuzzi could help alleviate your pain."

"It's funny, but that did occur to me as well...however, it's too soon. I couldn't go and sit in that Jacuzzi with the picture of Olive still clear in my head. I think I'll just stick to our walk-in bathtub. When we bought this house, I thought that was an unnecessary extra that we didn't need. Who knew?"

"If you're okay, then, I'll be going."

"Yes, I'm fine. You do what you have to do. I don't have any big plans. I'll just be lying here, trying to catch up on my German."

She tried to sound calm, but Adam knew her too well. He had the strong suspicion that she wasn't as involved with German grammar as she wanted him to believe. No, that enigmatic smile she gave him meant only one thing. She was going over all the events of the past week, trying to find some pattern, some clue that might help unravel the mystery that occupied all her waking moments. Despite his concern, Adam was reluctant to confront his wife and simply said, "Good. You stay here and rest. I won't be long." He looked at Eve who began to fidget with the blanket and hoped it was safe to leave her alone. He hated to do it, but he was anxious to locate the Wentworths before they left town and do some investigating of his own.

Adam had tried to put all the disagreeable business surrounding Olive's death out of his mind, but the discovery of Raul's body had been more than he was willing to accept. While there might still be lingering questions about Olive, it was clear that Raul had been murdered. Despite his advice to Eve to stop prying into other people's lives, he now began to take the opposite course of action. The Wentworths might know something important, he rationalized. They had, after all, been in the house across the street from the pool the morning Olive died. Adam wasted little time leaving the house and five minutes later, he set out for the Villas.

Eve had to confess that she wasn't terribly shocked by the news the deputy sheriff had brought them. Saddened, yes, but in a way, she'd suspected that something unfortunate had befallen Raul. Now, there was no longer any doubt. How sordid everything was becoming! A killer was on the loose in Sunshine Valley and little effort was being made to find him, or her. With great difficulty, she tried to push the troubling thoughts out of her mind. She was somewhat annoyed with Adam. How could he be thinking of stamps at a time like this? Weren't there more important things to consider? If only her body didn't ache so much, she would get out there herself and try to find out who killed Olive and Raul.

After a few minutes, Eve could no longer tolerate her restlessness. *Better to move around than to lie here helpless,* she thought, as she raised herself out of bed. She limped over to the hall closet and tried to find a light wrap that she could throw over her shoulders. As she was looking for a particular sweater, she spotted something rolled up in a ball and tossed into a corner on the floor. Bracing herself against the wall, she bent over and picked up a damp terrycloth robe that belonged to Adam. Judging from the smell, she assumed it must have been lying there for quite some time. She shook the wet garment, then brought it out to the patio and hung it on the clothes line to dry.

When the doorbell rang, Eve considered ignoring it. But, whoever it was persisted long enough to arouse her curiosity. She slowly made her way inside and opened the front door.

It was Pearl Thomas.

"I knew you were home," she said quietly, "but, I thought maybe you didn't hear me."

For a second, Eve thought something was wrong. Then she noticed the heavy dish in the woman's hands.

"I brought you a rice pudding," the woman said, holding out her arms.

Eve accepted the offering. "Thank you. This is lovely...but you shouldn't have."

"It was the least I could do," replied Pearl as she followed closely behind Eve into the kitchen. She seemed hesitant, but eager to talk. "How are you feeling?" she asked. "I heard about your accident. terrible thing to happen, You didn't break anything, did you?" Pearl hesitated as she spoke.

"No, Pearl. I'm okay, thank goodness. It could have been a lot worse. These old bones aren't as limber as they used to be. The doctor said it may take some time to fully recover, but, overall, I'm fine."

"Lucky you...didn't break anything."

"True." Eve had the strong sensation that there was something else on Pearl's mind. She looked at her questioningly, struck by the woman's unusual cheerfulness. This was not the same person she'd encountered the other day, someone who was so distraught and overcome by fear that she was capable of breaking into a neighbor's house.

"I suppose you heard about Raul?" she asked diffidently.

"Yes," Eve answered, putting the casserole in the refrigerator. "Deputy Warner stopped by the house. He told us."

"Deputy Warner? Why did he come?" For an instant, Pearl sounded alarmed. She looked at Eve with more than idle curiosity.

"Because of my accident. He wanted to know how I was doing and if I'd seen the driver of the truck."

"Oh, yes...of course," she snapped. "Well, I'd say...that's justice...after all."

It took Eve a moment to realize that Pearl seemed much more interested in Raul's death than in her accident. "What do you mean?" she asked.

"Raul got what was coming to him...he got what he deserved...you can't just go and kill somebody and expect...to get away with it," she stated haltingly, but firmly.

Eve blinked. Did she hear correctly? Why, she wondered, did her neighbor think that Raul killed Olive? "What makes you think Raul killed Olive?" she asked, giving voice to her thoughts.

"Well, he had...the opportunity...and a motive." She was very quick to respond.

Eve sensed that, for some unknown reason, Pearl appeared greatly relieved about something. "But, what makes you think someone actually killed Olive?" she asked, hoping her neighbor had more to say.

Pearl was stunned by the question, unable to answer at first. Then, she began stammering even more than usual. "I don't know...I just...figured it had to be...him."

"But, nobody has said anything about murder. Why do you think Olive was murdered? Her death was ruled an accident and I don't think anything has changed yet. At least I haven't heard anything to the contrary." Despite Eve's own suspicions, she did not want to share any of them with this woman.

Pearl began to backtrack. "I didn't mean to say that...maybe I'm wrong...maybe she wasn't killed." In spite of the hesitation, her voice had a hollowness to it, like someone burdened with guilty knowledge.

Eve drew closer to her neighbor. She wanted to make certain the woman understood everything she was about to ask her. "Now, listen to me, Pearl. This is important. I want you to tell me...is there something you failed to mention before?" Eve's voice was firm.

"Before?" Pearl began to squirm and slowly backed away from Eve.

"Did you see something that morning that you want to tell me about...something you didn't tell me before?" Eve persisted.

"No...no. I didn't see anything...I couldn't have seen anything." Pearl's voice began to tremble.

Here we go again, thought Eve. This seemingly innocent woman certainly appeared to have more than her share of secrets. "I think you better tell me everything you know, Pearl. It might be important...worse...it might be dangerous." Now that she'd gone this far, Eve had no intention of letting her neighbor off the hook.

"Dangerous? What do you mean?" Pearl sounded alarmed.

"Yes. You could be accused of withholding evidence. Even worse, if you saw or heard something and Olive was actually killed by someone, your own life might be in danger." Eve took advantage of Pearl's fear to prompt a confession and it worked.

"Well, I suppose you're right," Pearl began, slowly, "As I told you...I followed Olive to the pool."

Eve suspected she was in for a long story and was starting to feel uncomfortable standing in the kitchen. "Wait a minute," she said, putting up her hand to stop the woman. "I'm having difficulty...it's my legs...let's go into the living room and sit down."

Eve led the way, closely followed by Pearl. When they were comfortably seated opposite one another, Eve signaled for the woman to continue, hoping she hadn't lost her train of thought.

"As I started to say, I followed Olive to the pool that morning...that part is true."

She paused and looked at Eve for approval.

Eve nodded and smiled reassuringly at the woman. "Go on," she urged, "tell me...what happened next?"

"Well...you see...I didn't turn around and go back home...I went in...actually. I didn't use the front gate, but went around to the back entrance...that's where I saw Raul working along the wall. He saw me, but didn't smile as he usually did when we'd meet. He didn't look at all happy. Olive's back was turned when I went in and she didn't see me. I was so afraid...I was trying to get up the courage...to confront her. Then, all of a sudden...I heard the front gate open. I thought it was Raul and I didn't want him to hear what I was going to say...so, I quickly ducked into the dressing room and hid in the...shower stall. You can't imagine how stupid I felt...hiding like a silly school girl. I just stood there quietly and waited...hoping no one else would come in and see me."

"Was it Raul who opened the gate?" asked Eve.

"I never actually saw who it was, but I heard Olive start to shout. She said she was going to report him. I told you this too...and it's true...I don't remember her exact words, but, it had to do with something...illegal. Although I didn't see him, I just assumed she was yelling at Raul and that she was threatening to report him for being here illegally..."

Pearl stopped abruptly and looked to Eve for confirmation. Receiving none, she questioned, "Who else...could it have been?"

"What else did you hear, Pearl? Think! This is important." Eve pressed the woman.

"After a few minutes, I heard something that sounded like a scuffle...Olive began to scream...she said 'take your filthy hands off of me'...then, there was nothing...just silence. A few seconds later...I heard a big splash...then, everything went quiet. Oh, Eve, my heart was pounding. I thought I was going to faint. I heard the pool gate open and close. I waited...I don't know how long...before I dared to leave the shower. When I finally did come out, I looked around...nobody was there. That's when I saw her."

"Olive? You saw Olive?"

"Yes...in the Jacuzzi. Her head was under water...her eyes were closed and she looked dead, or at least unconscious."

Pearl was visibly shaken by having to recall all the events that led up to Olive's death. The vein on her neck begin to throb.

"Tell me, what did you do then?" Eve urged.

"I couldn't stand to look at her body...she looked grotesque...so I turned on the timer...the water started bubbling."

"Why, Pearl? Why did you do that? What reason would you have for turning on the timer?" Eve demanded.

"I don't know...maybe I wanted it to look like an accident...maybe I was afraid somebody might think I...did it...I don't know. All sorts of bad thoughts were running through my head, so, after the water started bubbling, I ran out as fast as I could. I was so cold my teeth...were chattering. When I got home and managed to calm down a little, I thought of calling the police...but, then I saw you and Adam leaving your house to go to the pool. I knew you would find her if...somebody hadn't already found her. I knew you would do the right thing...so, I just collapsed in a chair..."

"And you're sure you didn't hear the other person's voice?" Eve asked solemnly.

"No...I'm sure. I didn't hear anyone else. I only heard Olive."

So, that was it, thought Eve. Pearl had been at the pool when Olive was killed. There certainly was no doubt about it now. Her death wasn't an accident and it wasn't suicide. But, what Pearl didn't realize was that Olive wasn't yelling at Raul. Eve leaned back in her chair. She tried to picture Olive dying. How long did the killer have to hold her head under water? Did he watch her as she struggled? They were morbid questions, but, she tried to imagine how it was possible for someone to actually kill another person. She looked at Coco who was totally preoccupied with a rubber toy. She wished Adam would come home.

"Pearl," began Eve, after a long pause, "I want you to go home now. You need to stay inside and don't talk to anyone and, by all means, don't tell anyone what you just told me, at least, not yet. Adam and I will come over to your house. We'll have to call the police. Don't worry. You won't have to do it alone...we'll be there to help you."

The woman who'd appeared so elated a few minutes earlier, began to cry.

"Try not to get too upset, Pearl," Eve said. She felt that any words of sympathy would be inappropriate at this time and was eager to usher the woman out of the house. "All you have to do is tell the truth, the same as you just told me. But, please, don't say anything to anyone until Adam and I come over."

"All right, Eve...I'll be waiting for you," she sobbed as she went out the front door.

That explains why Pearl had seemed so relieved, Eve reflected. She'd been a witness to murder and was afraid she would be implicated. When she thought the killer had been found dead himself, she felt that she was off the hook.

Eve had barely time to cross the room, when the doorbell rang again. She wondered what Pearl could want this time. "Oh, Frank...I thought it was someone else," Eve said with a sigh of relief as she opened the door and saw her neighbor.

Frank Howell was holding a small bouquet. "I hope I'm not disturbing you," he said, shyly. "Please...these are for you. I heard about your accident." He reached out and handed the flowers to Eve, who had no choice but to accept the gift. She couldn't get over all the attention she was receiving. She smiled at Frank and asked him to come inside, explaining that Adam would be home any minute.

"I won't stay long. I just dropped by to see how you were doing," he said nervously, as he shifted his weight from one leg to the other.

Eve turned and went into the kitchen to get a vase.

"I suppose you heard about Raul," he shouted after her.

When Eve reentered the living room, Frank was smiling. She couldn't help but make the comparison with Pearl. Was he also relieved that Raul had been found dead?

"Yes, Frank. We heard this morning."

"A shame, don't you think?" The slight grin on his face belied his attempt to sound concerned.

"Yes, Frank, it is a shame." *What was it,* Eve wondered, *that Adam liked about this man?* Or, for that matter, what did Doty and Paula see in him? She found him rather cloying. Not one to beat around the bush, Eve decided to deal with her neighbor head on.

"Forgive me, Frank, but you seem rather pleased that they found Raul's body," she said, without any attempt to be tactful.

A flush of red spread over the man's face. "Pleased? Well, I wouldn't say I'm pleased. Grateful, maybe, that the man who killed my wife got what he deserved."

"Not you too? What makes you think Raul killed Olive? You never said anything about this before."

"People have been talking, you know..."

Was that it? Were his suspicions based on gossip? Or, did he too know something that he was reluctant to reveal? Eve wanted to know more. "To your knowledge, did Olive ever threaten Raul? Did you ever hear her threaten to turn him in to the police because he was here illegally?"

Frank had difficulty stifling a laugh, then replied. "Did she threaten him? Who didn't she threaten? I'm afraid that was her biggest problem, Eve. Nobody was safe. If she had only minded her own business and kept her mouth shut, she might still be alive today."

Eve was less than satisfied with Frank's answer, but decided not to press him further. She thought how remarkable it was that this man, who, a few days earlier, had been so remorseful over the fact that he might have inadvertently contributed to the death of his wife, was now almost gleeful at the prospect of being able to unload his burden of guilt onto someone else. She wished Adam would come home. He would know how to deal with Frank, for she was not entirely convinced that he was as innocent as he appeared to be.

"You seem to be feeling better," she said, with a hint of sarcasm.

Frank wiped his forehead with a handkerchief and looked at Eve with unexpected seriousness. "Eve," he said in a voice that was barely audible, "there's something I've been meaning to tell you that I feel you should know."

What else could there be? Eve wasn't certain she was ready for more bad news. To her great surprise, Frank began a lengthy confession about how he had, over a period of some months, been putting Valium in his wife's coffee. He further admitted that he thought perhaps he was, in some way, responsible for her death. But, he added, he never would have intentionally killed her. He simply wanted to make her life easier. He claimed he didn't know whether or not someone actually did kill Olive, but acknowledged that it was entirely possible. He only thought of Raul since she'd been threatening to turn him in and other people seemed to be pointing the finger at him as well.

Eve wondered who these 'other people' were that Frank was referring to and suspected that Doty and Paula had played some part in helping to alleviate his guilt. But, she was still somewhat perplexed. Why did Frank feel a need to make this confession to her? Perhaps he really was remorseful. He certainly gave that impression as he stood there perspiring and searching for the right words to make clear how he felt.

"But," Eve asked after a few moments, "what I still don't understand is, where did you get the Valium? I was under the impression that Olive didn't take prescription drugs. Was it your medicine?"

Frank hesitated. Apparently, there was more that he needed to divulge. He raised his eyebrows and let out a sigh, then slowly began to explain how he'd helped himself to the Valium he found at Doty and Paula's house. They always had a bottle of the pills standing on the counter or on a table. With great difficulty, he told Eve how he would help himself to a few tablets every time he went to their house. He didn't ask permission or tell them what he was doing, but was certain they wouldn't mind.

All of a sudden, Eve felt she'd gone too far. She found no pleasure in listening to the confessions of others. Although Frank continued to describe in detail how he took the tranquilizers and then administered them to his wife, she felt she didn't want to hear any more. "Stop," she said abruptly. "I really don't think you need to tell me all of this."

Frank stood there with his mouth open, uncertain what he should do next. He was saved from making this decision by the doorbell.

"Goodness," Eve exclaimed, "I'm certainly getting a lot of company today." She tried to appear cheerful as she opened the door and it wasn't difficult. In walked Doty and Paula, beaming from ear to ear.

"Hello, Eve. We've come to lift your spirits," said Paula in her most upbeat tone.

She led the way, followed by Doty, who was carrying a plate covered with tin foil.

"I didn't have a chance to bake that chocolate cake yet, but here are some cookies for you." Doty practically flung the plate at Eve. She uttered a weak "thank you," but felt unprepared for another gift.

The two women noticed Frank who'd receded to the couch. There was a moment of awkwardness as the three of them recognized and greeted each other.

'Well," said Paula, in an unusually effusive tone, "it's good to see you, Frank."

The three neighbors exchanged pleasantries, laughing and giggling at each other's remarks. They displayed an air of lightheartedness that Eve found astonishing and, she had to admit, somewhat sad. Who could have predicted that Raul's death might have such a positive effect on people? She could understand why people might be glad Olive was gone, but, Raul?

"Listen to me," Eve interrupted. "I know you all seem relieved that Raul's body was discovered..." She held up her hand to ward off their protests and continued. "I don't care about your reasons and I don't mean to stifle your enthusiasm, but, I think we should wait until the whole truth comes out."

"What do you mean?" Doty asked.

Paula looked at Eve, uncertain if she'd heard correctly. Frank simply shrugged his shoulders. "You know very well..." she began .

"What do I know, Paula?" Eve didn't let her finish.

"You know very well," continued Paula, "that Raul killed Olive. Isn't it obvious?"

Frank looked down. His face was flushed.

"You really believe that Raul killed her?" Eve asked.

"Yes, he did. He's the one who killed her." The conviction in Paula's voice left no room for doubt.

"And what was his motive?" continued Eve.

"Motive? What do you mean?" Paula asked, incredulously.

"Well, a person usually has to have a pretty good reason to kill someone else," Eve asserted.

"He had a perfect motive. He was here illegally. Even though everyone knew that, Olive was the only one who threatened to turn him in." Paula's conviction left no room for doubt.

"Hmm...yes...everyone knew that. She'd also threatened him before, right Frank?" Eve turned to Frank for confirmation. He looked up and nodded in agreement.

"Well, I'm afraid that's not good enough. I don't think for a minute that Raul killed Olive." Eve's voice was firm.

Paula appeared to falter for a second, then regained her composure. "You don't think Olive's death was an accident, do you?" she asked.

"I didn't say that," replied Eve.

"Well, what do you mean, then Suicide? Do you think Olive killed herself?" Paula asked petulantly. Her anger wasn't directed at Eve personally. It merely reflected her state of inner turmoil.

"No, it wasn't suicide. Olive was not the type of person to commit suicide, of that I'm quite certain. I think Olive was killed, but not by Raul," continued Eve.

"By who then?" asked Paula.

"I'm not sure who killed her, but I don't believe Raul did it."

"But, I heard him," Doty protested feebly, looking to Paula for support.

"Did you? Did you really hear Raul?" asked Eve. "You told me you just heard Olive yelling at someone that you believed to be Raul. You didn't actually see him or even hear his voice, right?"

Doty looked sheepish. She had nothing more to say. Eve stared intently at her three neighbors and had the impression they were watching each other as well. As usual, Doty's hands started to twitch, but Paula met Eve's penetrating look head on. Frank gazed fondly, first at Doty, then at Paula, then settled on the younger woman. When their eyes met, they both quickly looked away. Was there a hint of suspicion that passed between them, Eve wondered? Or, was it that they felt awkward about their feelings for one another?

When Eve was a teacher, she had a way of seeing through the pretenses of her students. If someone was guilty of a wrongdoing, the individual would sooner or later be forced into making a confession, unable to endure the discomfort of her seemingly all-knowing stare. But, unfortunately, this wasn't the classroom. Eve was perplexed. She couldn't tell if all three of these people were guilty or if they were all innocent. Didn't they each have a real motive for wanting Olive dead? An opportunity? Except for Frank, unless...

"Well, none of us has anything to hide, right?" It was Frank, surprisingly, who now took the lead. The two women agreed emphatically with his assertion, but the tension finally proved too much for Paula who got up and began pacing.

Eve was struck by the bond of intimacy that seemed to have developed among the three of them. She was touched by the way they appeared to care for one another. She even began to think differently about Frank. It had taken courage for him to confess to her that he'd stolen the Valium from Doty and Paula and that he'd been putting it in Olive's coffee on a regular basis. His admission had been totally unexpected and even though it made her uncomfortable, she admired him for it.

The room seemed to become warmer. Little by little, Eve's impatience was turning to anxiety. Where was Adam? Surely, he couldn't still be involved with his stamps.

Frank wiped the perspiration from his forehead and began rolling up his shirtsleeves. He was obviously hot. His arms were whiter than Eve would have thought for a person who plays so much golf.

"Perhaps we should go," Paula said, breaking the awkward silence. "You need your rest, Eve. You've been under too much stress."

"You're right. Maybe I do need to lie down for a while." Eve welcomed the opening and got up to show her neighbors out.

Once she was alone, Eve walked out to the patio to take in the robe that she'd hung up earlier. She saw Frank who was passing by, on his way back home. He waved to her as he crossed the pathway. Then, suddenly, Eve remembered something she'd completely forgotten. A rush of new images flooded her mind as she recalled the last time she'd seen a man with rolled up shirt sleeves wave to her.

"Voila! Of course," she exclaimed triumphantly, "That's it!" She was stunned by her own thoughts. Why didn't she see it before? Slowly, everything started to fall into place. Although she wasn't sure about the motive, Eve now knew who killed Olive. *Oh, Adam,* she thought, *where are you?*

Chapter 13

It took Adam about fifteen minutes to reach the Villas. He arrived just as the Wentworths were leaving for a trip to Nogales. Paul Wentworth, a tall handsome man in his early sixties, answered the door and asked Adam to come in. His wife, Janet, a much younger woman, was standing in front of the hall mirror, adjusting a pair of turquoise earrings.

"Nice jewelry," said Adam. He tried to sound friendly without being too solicitous. The woman turned and smiled. "I found these last Saturday at the open air market on Bolero Square. A Native American man has a little stand where he sells silver and turquoise jewelry that he's made. I believe he's from the Pima tribe. I got this bracelet there too," she said as she waved her arm at Adam.

"My wife loves Indian jewelry. I'll have to tell her." After he introduced himself, Adam began to explain the reason for his visit. "I'm sorry to disturb you, but this won't take very long," he added, apologetically. .

"Is there something we can do for you?" the man asked.

"It's about the house you were looking at a week or so ago...the one on Camino Avion—Bill Wells' place."

A look of recognition crossed the man's face. "Oh, yes, we really liked it," he said.

"Are you a realtor?" the man's wife asked, suspiciously.

"No...no. Nothing like that. I live down the block...on the same street. I was just wondering if you happened to notice anything odd when you went to look at the house. You know, a woman drowned in the pool that morning..." Adam chose his words carefully, knowing he'd have to be careful when questioning the Wentworths, so as not to upset them.

"Yes, we heard about that," interrupted the woman. "That's one reason we decided not to buy the place."

"That's right," her husband added. "We really liked the house, but after that woman died, we changed our minds. Janet thought it was a sign. Maybe she was right. Anyway, better safe than sorry. There are plenty of other places for sale here...we're still looking."

The man put his arm around his wife and they both smiled at each other.

"Can I get you something to drink?" the woman offered, extending her smile to Adam.

"No thank you, I know you're eager to get going and I don't want to take up too much of your time. I just have a few questions I'd like to ask you." Adam had taken an immediate liking to the couple. He sensed that they were deeply devoted and loyal to one another. That, he thought, was the essence of real love. It took him a moment to realize that they were waiting for him to continue.

"Did you happen to notice anything out of the ordinary that morning?" Adam asked.

"I'm not sure I know what you mean." The man looked puzzled.

"Did you see any unusual activity at the pool?" continued Adam.

"No," replied Paul Wentworth. "We were only interested in the house. We didn't even go over to the pool. I suppose we should have taken a look, but we didn't."

"Right," added his wife. "We arrived late for our appointment. All the streets look alike, so we had a difficult time finding the right one. When we finally found the house, we saw Dave's car. He must have been waiting for us."

"That's right. I remember we got out of the car and were going to ring the bell, but then we saw him crossing the street. He was coming from the pool and..."

"What did you say?" interrupted Adam. "Would you mind saying that again?"

The man repeated the same words. Dave Wilcox had just come from the pool and was crossing the street when they arrived at the house. His words seemed to hang in the air.

"He told us he was testing the water," Janet volunteered.

"Yes, that's right. He was carrying his suit jacket and said he got it wet, so he took it off and had to hang it up in his car to dry."

Adam listened intently as the man continued. "Dave's a strange fellow...nice enough, but you know how real estate agents can be. Actually, though, he surprised us."

"Oh? How so?" asked Adam.

"We were all set to make an offer on the house, but he told us, confidentially, of course, he thought the price was too high. Isn't that a new one? Usually, these fellows can be kind of pushy and want you to buy anything. They never tell you anything negative, but not Dave...just the opposite. He said it was noisy there too, on account of the pool. He thought we could get a better deal somewhere else and said he'd be happy to show us some other places."

"Yes, and when we heard about the drowning, that did it for me," added Janet. "I didn't need any more convincing."

Stunned by what he'd just heard, Adam thanked the couple for their help. They looked at him, puzzled, unable to comprehend the reason for the questions or the significance of what they had said.

"Now, I'll let you go," said Adam as the three of them exited the house. "I've taken up enough of your time." He stopped, then turned and thanked them again. "Have a good time in Nogales. It's a beautiful drive and I think you'll really enjoy the town. My wife and I went there a couple of months ago. It's fun...lots of unusual things to buy. We had lunch at a terrific restaurant...Benito's. You might want to try it. It's just over the border and they have fabulous Mexican food."

The couple smiled and said they would look for the restaurant. Adam walked over to his car and slid into the front seat. He sat behind the steering wheel for a few moments, reviewing what he'd just heard from the Wentworths. He was pleased with himself and thought he had reason to be. Nevertheless, he felt a slight sinking feeling in his stomach, a vague apprehension, realizing what he had to do next.

Despite her physical discomfort, Eve began pacing back and forth across the living room and looking out the window. Adam had promised that he wouldn't be gone long, but that was over an hour ago. However, she knew that once he got involved in a discussion about stamps, he might lose all track of time and she wouldn't see him for hours. *Of all times for him to be gone*, she thought.

As she approached the window for the fourth time, she noticed Dave Wilcox who was just pulling into their driveway. A feeling of panic came over her. Terrified, her mind started racing. What was he doing here? This was one person she had no desire to face alone, so she decided not to answer the door. He wouldn't know she was home by herself. After all, the car wasn't in the driveway. She stood motionless, holding her breath, as the doorbell rang. She put her finger to her mouth, hoping Coco wouldn't start barking, but that was a useless gesture. The dog began to bark loudly at the door, as Eve quietly backed her way into the rear of the house.

The doorbell rang again. Then, a third time. Coco was howling. After a few minutes, there was just silence. *Thank goodness he's gone*, thought Eve. Her heart was pounding. Then, all of a sudden, she heard a voice call out.

"Hello...is anybody home?"

Coco began barking again and Eve gasped. The patio door, she remembered. She'd left it unlocked when she went out to get Adam's robe. Oh my God! Dave Wilcox was standing in her living room.

"Hello," Eve responded, slowly making her way into the living room. "Oh, Dave. I didn't hear you come in. Is there something I can do for you?"

"I heard about your accident, so I thought I'd stop by to see how you're feeling and bring you some fruit."

Eve had been too frightened to notice that Dave was holding a basket filled with apples. He set it down on the coffee table while he continued to talk. "I rang the bell, but you probably didn't hear me," he said, in an attempt to excuse his entrance.

"No," Eve answered feebly. "I was in the back, lying down."

"The patio door was open..." he said haltingly.

"Yes, I see." *What was it he really wanted?* Eve wondered. Her mind was racing. Did he suspect she knew that he was the one who killed Olive? Why would he think that? So many thoughts raced through her mind and she began to tremble.

"You better sit down," said Dave, approaching her.

"No...no. I'm fine." She backed away from him, trying to collect herself.

"I thought I might find Adam here," said Dave.

"Adam? No, he's not here now, but I expect him back any minute."

Dave was rocking back and forth on his feet. With his right hand, he began jangling a pocket full of change. Next to whistling, it was a habit Eve found particularly annoying in men. Slowly, any apprehension she'd felt earlier, was replaced by anger.

"Why do you want to see Adam?" she asked boldly.

"I heard he called the office and was looking for me. I thought he wanted to talk about something."

"I'm afraid I don't know anything about that," she said abruptly.

"You're not thinking of selling this place, are you?"

"Absolutely not," replied Eve.

The man seemed uncertain whether to stay or leave. Eve's courage mounted. Before she fully realized what she was doing, she began her own line of attack.

"I see you're wearing your jacket today," she exclaimed.

Dave seemed surprised by the remark and looked down at his light green sport's coat.

"I always wear a jacket," he replied.

"Really? Are you sure about that? You weren't wearing a jacket the morning Olive was killed," Eve stated flatly.

Dave was stunned by her words. "What do you mean...*killed*?" he asked incredulously. "I thought her death was an accident...and what does my jacket have to do with anything?"

"When Adam and I were going to the pool, you waved to us. I remember you weren't wearing a jacket and your shirt sleeves were rolled up," Eve began to explain.

"So what? It was probably warm out. I roll up my sleeves all the time," he countered.

"Why aren't they rolled up now? It's hot out...much hotter than it was that morning. In fact, it was a very cold morning."

"You really have it in for me, don't you?" Dave looked at Eve and laughed, as if he were dealing with a lunatic who needed to be humored. He stopped jangling the coins in his pocket and began to rub his hands on the sides of his pants.

"Never mind. I think I already know the answer to my question...and so do you," Eve stated, her voice filled with contempt.

"I have no idea what you're talking about," replied Dave.

"Oh, yes you do...I think you got your sleeves wet when you struggled with Olive and pushed her into the Jacuzzi...there...I said it...I think you got your sleeves wet when you killed Olive."

"You're crazy." Dave began pacing.

"Really?" Eve asked, ignoring his insult. "What did she have on you, anyway?"

"You nosy busybody. You should mind your own business." The tone in his voice was becoming increasingly hostile as he moved towards Eve.

"What do you intend to do now? Kill me too? Like you killed Olive? And Raul? You killed him too, didn't you? Did he see you when you murdered Olive? Is that why? What are you going to do, kill everybody?"

Not waiting for Dave to respond to her accusations, Eve rattled off one question after another. She heard herself talking faster and faster as she backed across the room.

"There was another witness, you know," she said. Her ploy had worked. Dave stopped abruptly and Eve took the opportunity to run into the bedroom and lock the door behind her. He would have to break it down to get her and by the time he was able to do that, Adam would be home. At least, she hoped he'd be home. She still couldn't understand what was taking him so long.

Eve stood behind the locked door and waited quietly, blood rushing to her face and heart pounding. She'd even forgotten about her stiffness, but gasped when she felt a twinge of pain in her hip.

After what seemed an eternity, she heard someone calling her name. She looked at her watch and realized only fifteen minutes had passed. Was that Dave? Was he coming after her? Suddenly, there was a knock on the door and she felt herself become light-headed.

"Eve...it's me...are you in there?"

It was Adam.

Heaving a deep sigh of relief, Eve pushed the chair back and unlocked the door. She threw herself into her husband's arms. But, Adam was too preoccupied with his own news to suspect anything was wrong with his wife.

"Are you alone?" Eve asked, weakly.

"Yes, of course, I am...except for Coco, that is," he said as he pointed to the poodle who was pacing around nervously, obviously disturbed by the scene she had witnessed. "Listen, Eve," continued Adam. "I have something important to tell you. I know who killed Olive...and Raul."

"Dave Wilcox," Eve stated flatly. Her announcement was only a foreshadowing of what was to follow. "He was here...about fifteen minutes ago," she began.

"He was here? You let him in the house? Are you okay?" Eve's revelation was not something Adam had anticipated.

"I'm okay...physically, but I'm a bit upset... emotionally."

"He might have killed you." It was difficult to tell who was more upset, Adam or Eve.

"Would you mind calling the police?" Eve asked faintly.

"I already have. I stopped by the substation on my way home...that's why I'm late. They're going to pick him up."

"Oh, thank God," Eve said with a sigh of relief. She walked over to the couch, threw herself down and propped up her legs on the coffee table. Adam sat down next to her and slowly began to recount what he'd learned from the Wentworths.

Chapter 14

News of the discovery of Raul's body and subsequent arrest of Dave Wilcox spread quickly throughout Sunshine Valley. Fearing an increase in the crime rate, many residents took measures to protect themselves by installing wrought-iron bars on the doors and windows of their houses. Apparently, security seemed more important to a surprisingly large number of people than did freedom. Little by little, however, a sense of calm and serenity began to return to the once peaceful desert community. Nevertheless, the recent double murders would provide months of gossip-filled poolside conversation. Whether they liked it or not, Eve and Adam Iverson had become the focus of interest for many residents. Almost overnight, they'd become local celebrities. Today was no exception.

"I'm curious. When did you first suspect that Dave Wilcox was the killer?" Peggy Walsh asked Eve, who was reclining in a lounge chair by the pool.

"It took me a while, but something always bothered me about the morning Olive died. If you recall, it was very cold. I think it was when I found Adam's robe in the closet that it hit me. He'd worn it to the pool that morning and I remembered how he had to roll up his sleeve when he pulled out the thermometer to check the temperature of the water."

A crowd began gathering around Eve, eager to hear her account. She searched her memory, trying to make sure she didn't forget any important details, then took a sip of water from her glass and continued. "Adam and I saw Dave Wilcox when we were on our way to the pool. He wasn't wearing a jacket. He was just in shirt sleeves and they were rolled up. I remember thinking at the time that he must be awfully cold. I think I put this out of my mind until the day I found Adam's damp robe. Then, it hit me. All of a sudden, everything became clear. The reason Dave wasn't wearing his jacket when we saw him was that he'd gotten it wet. This happened when he pushed Olive in the Jacuzzi and held her head under the water...when he killed her..."

"And that's why he had to roll up his sleeves." Peggy finished Eve's narration for her.

"Precisely," added Eve.

"You are positively brilliant," said one onlooker. "I think you and Adam should open a detective agency. We could use one here."

"I'm afraid...or at least I hope...we wouldn't have much business," Eve added, smiling.

Everyone was curious to hear more. Was Eve scared to be alone in the house with Dave? What was Frank going to do now that he was single? What motive did Dave have for killing Olive? And what about Raul? Why did Dave kill him too?

As Eve continued her account of events, she explained what she and Adam learned from Deputy Warner. Dave Wilcox was arrested at his house as he was packing to leave town. He knew it wasn't going to take long before the authorities came after him, but he had no idea it would happen so quickly. His biggest problem was that he underestimated everyone. But, once Deputy Warner took him into custody and began questioning him, he started talking and made a full confession.

According to Deputy Warner, Dave had a somewhat checkered career. He'd been in Sunshine Valley for about five years and during that time, he did quite well.

He developed a good business and earned a rather decent reputation. However, before coming to Arizona, he lived in Florida and became involved in some shady financial dealings in which he preyed on rich widows. Over the years, he managed to swindle several women out of sizeable sums of money. He thought he'd left all that behind him, but, one of his victims would return to haunt him. Olive Howell had lived in Florida with her husband and, when he died, she became the target of one of Dave's fraudulent investment schemes and lost a great deal of money. Years went by. She left the state and probably thought she'd seen the last of Dave and her money until, one day, she recognized him in Sunshine Valley. She confronted him and threatened to expose his corruption. Even though the authorities in Florida were never able to get enough evidence to prosecute Dave, Olive could have ruined his business in Arizona by exposing his disreputable past and telling what she knew about him.

"So," Peggy asked, wide-eyed, "Dave killed Olive to keep her from talking?"

"Well, he maintains it was an accident. He saw Olive go into the pool that morning, but didn't follow her with the intent of killing her...or so he says. He wanted to talk to her, try to convince her to keep quiet. He said he'd even returned the money she claimed he stole from her...in cash...over ten thousand dollars. But, she wanted more and began to blackmail him. He started to give her what she wanted to keep her quiet, but soon realized her demands were not going to end and he couldn't afford to keep paying her. Dave claimed that when he went over to the pool to beg Olive to back off, she just kept yelling and threatening to expose him. He said he never pushed her, but that she was out of control when she slipped and fell on the concrete and knocked unconscious."

"If she fell on the concrete, how come you found her in the Jacuzzi?" Peggy asked wide-eyed.

"According to Dave's confession, he seized the opportunity and dragged her body over to the Jacuzzi. He wanted to make sure she didn't regain consciousness. He pushed her head under the water and held it down. That's how he got his arms wet. Then, realizing what he was doing, he panicked and ran out. He was afraid someone might see him, and...someone did."

"Raul?" Peggy guessed.

"Yes...and Dave saw him too as he ran out, but he couldn't deal with him at that moment. His appointment was waiting for him across the street...two people from Illinois. He quickly showed the couple through the house, but discouraged them from buying it. He feared that, when Olive's body was discovered, they'd remember seeing him come out of the pool and it would raise too many questions."

"What about Raul?"

"He still had to be dealt with. He was working outside the pool when Dave finished showing the house and probably didn't even know Olive was dead. But, Dave couldn't take any chances. Once Olive's body was discovered, he knew Raul could implicate him. So, he ran around to the back of the pool area and told him he had some work that needed to be done immediately for which he was willing to pay a hundred dollars. Raul dropped what he was doing, got into the car with Dave and they drove off. Dave lured Raul into his house and, when his back was turned, hit him over the head with an iron bar."

"I think they should change the name of this place to Death Valley," remarked one woman.

"Already taken," observed her husband.

"How can you joke about this? I think it's absolutely horrid," said Peggy.

"Yes, it is," said Eve and continued recounting the details of the murders. "It might be possible to say Olive's death was accidental. Dave adamantly maintains that he had no intention of killing her. But Raul...that was cold-blooded murder. After Dave knocked him unconscious, he tied a plastic bag around his head. Later that night, he dragged the body out to his car and drove into the desert, where he poured a bottle of tequila down Raul's throat and then dumped him."

"And nobody suspected anything, " said Peggy.

"When they discovered Valium in Olive's body and ruled her death accidental, Dave couldn't believe his good fortune. With her and Raul out of the way, he thought he was home free and was sure nobody would ever trace the dead bodies to him."

Eve was asked to repeat parts of her story and she answered one question after another. *It was an odd sensation to be the focus of so much attention*, she thought, especially when it was a question of murder. But, she wouldn't have been completely truthful if she didn't admit that, in a way, it appealed to her. What especially pleased her was the fact that she was finally able to solve a complex puzzle.

"I think you should write a book," said one woman.

"Oh, good heavens! Once was enough. I'd hate to have to go through the whole fiasco again. I'll leave the book writing to someone else. All of this has been exhausting for both me and Adam. And, right now, I'm worn out just having to talk about everything." After a short pause, Eve looked around and said, "If you'll excuse me, I really have to go home now." She put on her robe, gathered her belongings, then got up and made her way through the crowd to the pool gate.

When she arrived home and opened the front door, she was greeted by another surprise.

"Guess what?" Adam teased, waving an official looking letter in the air.

"Now what? I'm almost afraid to ask."

"They want to make us honorary deputy sheriffs."

Eve couldn't help but laugh. "Deputy sheriffs? You and me? Does that mean we get to wear badges too?"

Adam wasn't as amused as his wife. "I think it's kind of nice," he said sheepishly.

"Yes, dear, but promise me you won't wear your gun to bed."

"I'd have to buy one first."

Adam continued reading the letter while Eve went into the bathroom to shower and change clothes. When she finished, she walked out to the patio to hang up her bathing suit and towel. She glanced over at Frank's house. Music from inside the house filtered out to the street. This was not a sound Eve was used to hearing, at least not coming from Frank's house. He was entertaining. Doty and Paula appeared on the patio to check something that was cooking on the barbecue.

"Smells good," Eve shouted and waved to the two women.

"Ribs," responded Paula.

Well, thought Eve, *looks like Paula got her hearing aid*. There are worse things in life than having a large inheritance to spend. She wondered what Olive would have to say about the turn of events and concluded, "the meek shall inherit" was most appropriate.

As Eve turned to go inside, she noticed her neighbor Maggie marching briskly down the street. Ten seconds later, the front doorbell rang. When she came in from the patio, Maggie was already standing in the middle of the living room, beaming from ear to ear. Before either of the women had a chance to say a word, Adam excused himself and retreated to the rear of the house.

"Oh, Eve, I'm so glad I caught you at home."

"Maggie, I've been meaning to come over and talk to you, but so much has been happening..." Eve didn't have a chance to finish apologizing.

"Yes, I know. I heard. Awful business," said Maggie, but she had something more urgent on her mind that she wanted to discuss. Her smile disappeared. She took a deep breath and wrinkled her nose as if she smelled something unpleasant. "Do you remember that matter I discussed with you a couple of weeks ago?"

"I'm sorry, Maggie, but, with all that's happened, I haven't been much help in locating your vase."

"Well, not to worry. I don't want to trouble you any more. You can forget about it. Actually, you can forget about everything I told you."

"Really? Are you sure?" Eve asked quizzically.

"Yes...silly me...I finally remember what happened to that vase."

"You do?"

"Yes. I gave it to my daughter...when I went to see her. I was in such a hurry getting everything together, I forgot that I brought it with me."

"Oh...I see."

"Anyway, thank you for your help. I hope I wasn't a bother...but, you know how easy it is to forget things."

"Yes, I do. I'm so glad you found your vase, Maggie." *What a relief*, thought Eve. *Another mystery solved.*

Without uttering another word, the woman turned to leave. She paused for a moment as she held the door knob and turned her face towards Eve. "You know," she said, "to tell you the truth, I never really thought Pearl could do such a terrible thing as to steal my vase. She's not the type. I'm so glad I was right."

The woman had no sooner left when the doorbell rang again. Had she forgotten something? Was there another problem? For a moment, Eve felt that her sense

of relief might be premature. But, when she opened the
door, she was surprised to see a young Mexican man
standing there, dressed in a suit, hair combed neatly
back.

"Senora Iverson?" he asked with a note of hesitation.

"Si," answered Eve.

The man awkwardly extended a small bouquet and
muttered something resembling an apology. Eve didn't
understand what he was saying and wasn't sure what to
make of the gesture, but she accepted the flowers he
was offering and thanked him. Then, she spoke to him
in Spanish, explaining that she didn't understand the
reason for the lovely gift. He grew more comfortable
when he realized he could speak in his native language
and confessed that he was the one who was responsible
for her accident. He said that he had put in a lot of
hours that day and was anxious to get home because it
was his sister's birthday. He apologized profusely and
asserted that he didn't see Eve and didn't even realize
he had almost hit her until he heard about it the next
day. He would have come to see her earlier, but was
scared, afraid he might get in trouble. When he told his
mother what had happened, she insisted that he do the
right thing. After several polite exchanges, Eve
reassured the young man that she was all right and then
thanked him for being so thoughtful.

"Who brought the flowers?" Adam asked when he
returned to the living room.

"The young man who was driving the truck that
almost hit me. He came to apologize, but I forgot to ask
his name."

"I wish you'd let me know," said Adam. There are a
few things I'd like to say to him."

"Oh, you should have seen him. He was very polite
and so apologetic. He didn't mean to hurt me. I think
we should just let it go," countered Eve.

"Well, I'm glad he came after Maggie was here and not before."

"Why is that?" asked Eve, as she began arranging the flowers in a vase.

"She might have thought this was hers," Adam said, pointing to the green vase in which Eve had placed the flowers.

"Oh, dear," she said, taking a few steps backward. Eve started humming and Adam was pleased that his wife was in such good spirits again. "You know," she said, tying a multi-colored square cloth around her neck, "I think I'm going to enjoy being an honorary deputy after all...who would have thought?"

"Well, in that case, deputy Iverson," replied Adam, "I believe we have some unfinished business to take care of."

"Oh?"

"There's the matter of the body in Pearl's garden," he said somberly.

Eve paused and looked at her husband. "Good heavens...I'd completely forgotten about that."

"Well, not to worry. I don't think he's going anywhere, but we do need to contact the proper authorities...but later...not now. We have plenty of time." Eager to change the subject, Adam pointed to his wife's neck and said, "that's a pretty nifty scarf you're wearing."

"Bandana," Eve corrected and smiled. "It's part of adapting to local customs. Now, let's get out of here and go for a nice lunch. I think we deserve a treat after all we've been through and I don't want to answer any more doorbells."

"I must say, you've really made a remarkable recovery," said Adam as he smiled at Eve. "I was worried for a while, but now I can relax. And you're right, we deserve to treat ourselves."

Eve walked over to Coco who was resting in her wicker basket, exhausted from all the recent activity. She patted the dog on the head and said, "You stay here and guard the house, Coco. We won't be gone long." Then she took Adam's arm and they both went out the front door. The sun was shining, not a cloud in the sky, and everywhere she looked, Eve saw bright colors. "You know," she said, as they headed for the driveway, "this place can really grow on a person."

Once in the car, Eve turned to Adam and asked, "Where are we going to have lunch?"

"Well," said Adam, "I heard about a place called 'Crazy Cactus.' It's on the edge of town. They're supposed to have terrific food. I thought it would be fun to try a new place for a change."

"I'm game. It's already one o'clock and I'm starving...let's go."

As they drove down Camino Avion, they passed the community pool. A crowd of people was gathered around a news truck. A man with a camera was focusing on Deputy Bud Warner who was being interviewed, presumably by a reporter. Although someone from the local newspaper had come to the pool and interviewed a few people, this was the first time Eve and Adam saw television cameras.

"Keep driving," said Eve, as she ducked out of sight. "I don't want to have anything to do with this," she said emphatically. "I hope nobody saw us. Let's just get out of here." Adam accelerated towards the main road before anyone had a chance to flag him down. He too shared Eve's need to avoid any confrontation with the media.

"There's one thing I'd like to tell everyone, but I don't think I'm quite ready for TV," said Eve hesitantly.

"And, what might that be?"

"You might think this is crazy, but I really believe both my foreign language learning and my painting helped me discover who killed Olive."

"I'm intrigued. How so?"

"Well, one day when you were out on one of your stamp expeditions, I happened to see a program on television about the benefits of learning a foreign language. They said that it's very healthy for the brain. Not only does it increase memory and problem solving skills, but, the research shows that it also makes a person more perceptive and better at spotting misleading information."

"Just like Hercule Poirot," said Adam. "As I recall, he was multilingual."

"Right, and don't forget Sherlock Holmes and Charlie Chan."

"Ah so. Well, you're right up there with the top sleuths."

"I'm also quite certain that my interest in art helped me. I've always known that the act of painting increases a person's perception as well as the ability to retain visual information. I think that's why I focused so much on Olive's slippers and why I was able to so vividly recall Dave Wilcox in his shirt sleeves."

"Well, I must say, you really put your skills to good use."

"I just hope I don't have to use these skills to solve any more crimes."

As they continued toward the restaurant, Eve thought it might be time to address one last item related to Olive's death that had been lingering in her mind. She chose her words very carefully as she slowly began to recount what Peggy Walsh had told her regarding the accusation someone had made against the two of them.

Adam listened, but didn't say a word. He just smiled and continued driving.

"I didn't want to tell you earlier because I thought it would upset you. At least, now, we're off the hook."

"Well," replied Adam, "I heard the same rumor, not from Peggy Walsh, but from a man I ran into while walking Coco. He stopped me one day to thank me. When I asked him what I had done, he told me that some folks were saying that you and I were the ones who killed Olive and they were mighty grateful. I didn't want to tell you what I heard for the same reason you didn't want to tell me."

"I must say," replied Eve, "we certainly are two very considerate people." After a few silent moments, she turned to Adam and said, "This is really odd. It never even occurred to me that you might have had something to do with Olive's death. But, after Alice and I left the pool, you had quite a bit of time alone with her until the authorities arrived. If she wasn't already dead, you had ample opportunity to finish the job...Oh, dear, is it possible that, now, you too, like so many others in Sunshine Valley, have a secret?"

Adam smiled at his wife, but didn't say a word. As he passed the last big shopping mall, he finally turned to Eve. "There it is," he said, pointing to a restaurant that boasted a large sign in the shape of a cactus. He pulled into the busy parking lot and drove around twice before he found an empty space. "Now, let's put Olive behind us and focus on our lunch."

"You're right," said Eve, "Crazy Cactus certainly looks popular. It must be good."

After parking the car, she and Adam walked up the ramp and entered the restaurant. "Wow," said Adam, as he looked around. "I'd heard this was a popular place, but, I didn't think it would be this crowded. Wait here. I'll give the waitress our name...I hope it won't take too long to get a table."

When Adam returned, he pointed to a bench that had just been vacated. They walked over and sat down. "We're in luck," he said. "It's past the height of the lunch hour and a lot of people are getting ready to leave. She said it would only be about fifteen minutes. In the meantime, we can sit here, relax, and enjoy the ambience.."

"You have no idea how much I'm looking forward to this. After all the nonsense we've been through these past few weeks, I'm ready for something pleasant." Eve sat back and began to look around at the walls that were covered with a variety of desert landscape paintings. All of a sudden, her gaze stopped abruptly. "I don't believe this," she gasped as she pointed to one of the canvases that hung in a far corner. "Do you see what I see? Can it be? I'm not sure, but I think that's my cactus painting...the one that was stolen...it certainly looks like my style."

Adam stood up and walked into the restaurant to get a closer look at the painting. "You're right," he said, when he returned. "It has your signature on it."

"Oh no...I can't believe this. We have find the manager. I want to know what my painting is doing here..."

"Well, Deputy Iverson," said Adam, as he put his arm around Eve's shoulder, "it looks like we might have another case on our hands. I'll see if there's anyone here who can help us." He got up and slowly walked over to the cashier.

THE END

About the Author

Rita Strombeck has a Ph.D. in Scandinavian Studies and an M.A. in French from the University of Chicago. Like her heroine, Eve Iverson, she taught languages for several years and enjoys painting. In 1982, she started her own business. Over the years, she has developed more than 50 educational books and programs for health care professionals and the general public. Rita also received twelve grants from the National Institutes of Health (NIH) and has written successful grant proposals for various nonprofit organizations. She currently lives in Palm Springs and recently wrote an article for *Palm Springs Life* magazine about the city's early women entrepreneurs—"Women With Vision."

Ever since discovering Nancy Drew in 5th grade, Rita has been a fan of mysteries and now has decided to focus on this first love. She has written a children's book based on Sherlock Holmes. *Hot Tub of Death* is her first cozy mystery.